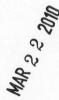

Library and Archives Canada Cataloguing in Publication

Polak, Monique

The middle of everywhere / written by Monique Polak.

ISBN 978-1-55469-090-9

I. Title.

PS8631.O43M54 2009   jC813'.6   C2009-903349-6

First published in the United States, 2009

Library of Congress Control Number: 2009929363

Summary: Noah spends a school term in George River, in Quebec's Far North, trying to understand the Inuit culture, which he finds both threatening and puzzling.

Orca Book Publishers gratefully acknowledges the support for its publishing programs provided by the following agencies: the Government of Canada through the Book Publishing Industry Development Program and the Canada Council for the Arts, and the Province of British Columbia through the BC Arts Council and the Book Publishing Tax Credit.

Design by Teresa Bubela
Cover artwork by Getty Images
Author photo by Monique Dykstra

ORCA BOOK PUBLISHERS   ORCA BOOK PUBLISHERS
PO Box 5626, STN. B   PO Box 468
VICTORIA, BC CANADA   CUSTER, WA USA
V8R 6S4   98240-0468

www.orcabook.com
Printed and bound in Canada.
Printed on 100% PCW recycled paper.

12 11 10 09 • 4 3 2 1

For Sapina and Joe

one

I bet I'm the only jogger in the history of George River. People up here don't jog or work out in a gym; they get exercise doing stuff like hunting seals or running from polar bears.

But it's my first full day in town and a run might help. It's pretty depressing being up here in the middle of nowhere, two plane rides away from Montreal. There's nothing to see except snow and more snow.

"Isn't it magnificent?" Dad said this morning when he opened the curtains. "Just have a look at that view, will ya? It's like waking up to a painting, is what it is."

What it also is is friggin' cold. I know, because Dad's obsessed with checking his computer for the weather report. "Are you sure you can handle this kind of cold?" he asked when he saw me lacing up my shoes. "I was online just now and it's minus twenty-eight Celsius, minus thirty-eight with the windchill factor." Dad whistled. Cold weather impresses him. "Your body's not acclimatized yet, Noah."

"I can handle it. And I can take Tarksalik. That way you won't have to walk her."

Dad liked that idea. It meant he had time for another coffee before his first class. And, who knows, maybe the temperature would drop another degree. That'd really get Dad's day off to a good start.

I've already run from Dad's apartment, past the airport to the dump where the road ends, and now I'm headed back. It's so quiet up here, it's creepy. All I can hear is the sound of my running shoes hitting the snow-covered road. I check my watch. A half-hour run should do me. Tomorrow, I'll add five minutes. One thing's for sure: working out sure beats sitting around, looking out the window at the snow and hanging out with the weatherman.

I hear the pickup truck before I see it.

It's coming from behind me, rumbling up the hill.

Tarksalik is about forty feet ahead of me, running by the side of the road. I can tell she's got sled-dog blood in her from the way she runs: head high, legs taut.

The sun has just come up, and when it lands on Tarksalik, it looks like she's shining too. For the first time since I found out I'd be spending this term in Nunavik, in northern Quebec, getting reacquainted with my dad, I don't feel one hundred percent miserable. Right now, as I let the fresh cold air fill my lungs, I'd say I'm down to about eighty-five percent miserable.

Maybe, I think as I watch Tarksalik run, this visit won't turn out to be a total disaster. Maybe there's more to life than Montreal.

On our way out to the dump, Tarksalik ran up into the tundra to sniff around the low bushes that grow there. George River is right at the tree line, so there aren't any real trees to speak of, just low bushes, spruce mostly. But now Tarksalik is back by the side of the road. Every so often, she turns to make sure I'm still there. Considering we only met yesterday, she's already pretty attached to me. That's dogs for you; always ready to make a new friend. Human beings, at least the ones I've met, are more complicated.

The truck's rumble comes closer. My body tenses. I could shout "Stay!" at Tarksalik, but I'm worried that the sound of my voice might make her turn around and run straight into the truck's path. Tarksalik isn't afraid of trucks or cars. Yesterday Dad gave her hell for chasing an SUV. Up here, dogs don't learn to fear vehicles the way city dogs do. There are hardly any cars or trucks in the frozen North. And that's because there's no place to go. There's only one road in town, and it goes round in a circle for about four kilometers.

Dad says he likes living where there's only one small road that doesn't really go anywhere. "Life's less complicated. And the air—there's nothing like it," he says. But I'd trade the fresh air for a highway that'd get me out of here.

In winter, people in George River mostly use snow-mobiles to get around. Just about everything gets shipped here from down south. Most stuff comes by plane, but bigger items, like cars, only get shipped in summer when Ungava Bay thaws. A carton of milk costs five bucks in George River, so you can imagine what a car would go for.

I'm thinking what an awful thing it'll be if Tarksalik gets hit by this truck. How bad I'll feel for offering to take her out with me in the first place. And what a lousy start it'll be for my stay in George River. But Tarsalik's not going to get hit. No way. I mean, what are the chances?

All of that is going through my head when the red pickup truck speeds up and drives past me. The driver waves at me. He has straight jet black hair, and he's sucking on a cigarette.

"Hey," I shout, pointing at the dog. But it's too late. The truck zooms ahead.

Tarksalik doesn't stay. Alerted by the sound of the truck's engine, she turns toward the road. Then, just like that, she runs out into the road, heading right for the truck. Her tail is wagging, like she expects something really good to happen.

Don't, I think. Please don't. Please. No.

But she does.

I hear a thud as Tarksalik's body makes contact with metal, followed by a terrible yelp. What happens next feels like it's in slow motion. Tarksalik's body flies into the air—it must go up five feet—and lands on the middle of the road. A dark pool forms in the snow around her. Blood. Sled-dog blood.

No matter how long I live, I know I'll never be able to wipe that moment from my mind.

"Tarksalik!" I cry out, choking on her name.

I'm sure the driver will stop. He must have felt Tarksalik's body when it hit the truck. He must have heard her yelping. If she's alive, he'll know what to do, where to take her for help.

But the bastard just keeps driving, leaving Tarksalik and me out there in the cold, a good two kilometers from town. I shake my fist in the air as the red pickup truck disappears behind a hill of snow. As far as I can tell, the heartless asshole doesn't even bother to look in his rearview mirror.

I've never run as fast as I do to reach Tarksalik. Please, God, let her be okay.

She is lying in a pool of blood, but I can't tell for sure where the blood is coming from. Maybe her mouth; maybe her rump. Her blue eyes are open, but there's a gray film over them, and her breath sounds raspy. When I reach down to touch her muzzle, she bites my hand. Her teeth tear through my fleece running mitts, breaking the skin underneath. Now I'm bleeding too.

I pull my hand away. If it hurts, I don't notice.

I know if I try to move Tarksalik, she'll bite me again. That means I've got to leave her in the middle of the road and hope no more cars or trucks come along.

I know I have to get help. Fast.

"Tarksalik," I say, looking her in the eye and trying not to cry, "I'm going to get Dad. You're going to be okay. I promise. I'll get a doctor."

I don't notice anything on my run back into town. The air must be sharp and cold, but I don't smell it. There's snow everywhere, and in the distance the George River is covered with a thick layer of pale blue ice, but I don't see it.

All I know is how I feel and what I'm thinking. My heart is sagging in my chest, weighing me down, but I have to keep running, moving one leg forward after the other. What if Tarksalik doesn't make it? What if—the thought makes me groan—some other car comes by and finishes what the truck started?

I have to get Dad. I have to get a doctor. I run faster than I've ever run. My throat and lungs burn from the cold. My knee joints ache.

That's when it occurs to me: there are no doctors in Kangiqsualujjuaq, which is the name of Dad's town, though everyone up here just calls it George River or sometimes even just George.

I heard Dad and a couple of the other teachers talking about it last night. The closest doctor is in Kuujjuaq, a half-hour plane ride away, ten hours by snowmobile. George River doesn't even have an X-ray machine.

What kind of godforsaken place have I come to, anyway?

TWO

I pound on the door of Dad's apartment. I have the key, but my fingers are too frozen to fish it out of my pocket. "It's Tarksalik!" I shout. "She got hit by a truck."

Dad opens the door. He's holding his toothbrush. His face is as white as the snowdrifts by the porch. "Is she dead? Where is she?"

"She's not dead. But she's bleeding bad. She wouldn't let me touch her. She's on the road—on the way out to the airport." I'm panting so much I can hardly breathe.

Dad throws on his parka. I smell coffee. "Go across the street to Steve's," Dad says, pressing his palm down on my shoulder. "Tell him we need him to help us get her."

Steve is Dad's closest friend up here. He's the principal at the school where Dad teaches. Steve's from Ontario, but his wife Rhoda is Inuit. She runs the daycare program at the school. They live with their five-year-old son Etua and

7

their daughter Celia, who's nine, in a prefabricated house like Dad's, only theirs isn't divided into two apartments the way Dad's is.

Etua answers the door. "Hey," he says, grinning up at me, "I got my Spiderman pj's on."

The house smells like pancakes. Steve is standing by the stove. He's still wearing his bathrobe. Rhoda is in the hallway, braiding Celia's hair. "Steve!" I call out. "Tarksalik got hit by a truck. We need you to help us get her. She's out on the middle of the road. On the way to the airport."

It is only afterward, after we've gone back for Tarksalik (who has managed somehow to drag herself to the side of the road) and I am crouched over her on the *qamutik* (a sled on two skis attached to Steve's snowmobile), that I realize Dad and Steve didn't panic. Not one bit. The two of them just sprang into action. They used a blanket to hoist Tarksalik onto the *qamutik*, then covered her with another blanket. A blue and black plaid blanket with blue fringes. It's weird the stuff you notice when you're in the middle of something awful.

When I talk to Steve later about how he and Dad didn't freak out, Steve looks surprised. "I've seen some bad stuff happen up here, Noah. We had a suicide at the school three weeks ago. And last year, Tilly Watts lost her hand in a snowmobile accident. We're out on the land, not in cars with seatbelts and airbags. When accidents happen out here, we can't afford to panic."

We bring Tarksalik straight to Mathilde's house. Mathilde's the town nurse. She works at the clinic, but because she and Dad are friends, Dad knows she has Tuesdays off.

Mathilde doesn't panic either, even when we turn up at her door with a bleeding dog. She lays Tarksalik out on her living-room floor, and she doesn't seem to notice when her beige carpet gets spattered with blood. Then she runs her hands along the length of the dog's body, feeling for breaks. Tarksalik yelps again, but Mathilde doesn't think there are any broken bones. "She's in shock. I'm going to the clinic to get her some pain meds. These first few hours are very important," she says.

Mathilde grabs her backpack. It's black with hot-pink and turquoise stripes, and it looks like it might be Mexican. There I go noticing weird stuff again.

A minute later, Mathilde is out the door and on her way to the clinic. Luckily, it's just down the road. She'll be back soon with the pain medication.

Dad is chewing on his lower lip. He loves that dog. Until I arrived in George River yesterday, Tarksalik was his only family up here. The dog was living outside when Dad first came to town. He used to feed her scraps, but then one really cold night, she came into Dad's apartment, and she's lived there ever since.

Tarksalik is the Inuktitut word for *spot*. Dad named her that because she's got a white spot on her forehead and because when Dad was learning to read, the dog in the reader they used at his school was named Spot. So Tarksalik's the Inuktitut version of that dog. "It's a bilingual play on words," Dad explained to me. "Get it?"

Tarksalik follows Dad everywhere, even when he takes a pee. Dad says she's the best pet he ever had. "Probably because she's so darned grateful," he told me.

Now Dad strokes the spot on Tarksalik's forehead. "You're going to be okay," he tells her, but his voice doesn't sound too sure.

"What can I do?" Sitting around watching Tarksalik, and watching Dad watch Tarksalik, is only making me feel worse. I need to *do* something.

"You'd better get to school, Noah," Dad says. He stops stroking Tarksalik to check his watch. "You've got forty minutes till the bell goes." He eyes my jacket. It's smeared with Tarksalik's blood. "There's time for you to clean yourself up, change your clothes. We're in room 218. Listen, tell the other kids I'm going to be a little late. And tell them to work on their compositions till I get there." Dad sounds less broken up when he talks about school.

Being back at Dad's apartment without Dad or Tarksalik for company feels weird. I stop to look at a picture of me on the living-room mantel. It must have been taken ten years ago, after Mom and Dad split up. I'm standing on one leg and my arms are spread out like wings. It looks like I'm pretending to be an airplane. Dad must have taken the picture when he got back from one of his trips and I went to meet him at the airport.

The blood on my jacket comes off with a little cold water and some scrubbing. I shower and toast myself a bagel and smear some peanut butter on it, but I can't stop hearing the thud Tarksalik's body made when the truck hit her or picturing Tarksalik flying up into the air or seeing the black puddle of blood.

If only I hadn't gone for a run. If only I hadn't offered to take Tarksalik. If only I hadn't come up north in the first place.

There's a No Boots rule at Dad's school. You have to leave your boots in the front hallway. It's a way to prevent tracking in snow. So the first thing I see when I walk into school is this long row of boots. I park mine at the far end. I'm glad there aren't any holes in my socks.

I already met some of Dad's students yesterday afternoon when I got off the plane from Kuujjuaq. Dad thought I might as well meet them right away, considering I was going to be in their class till June, when the school term ends.

"Not to worry," Dad told them after we'd all shaken hands, Inuit-style. Actually, from what I can tell, the Inuit don't shake hands, they just grab your hand and hold it, not pumping it up and down the way we do. "I'm not going to give Noah here any special treatment, even if he is my own son. Even"—Dad's voice went up a little, which meant he was about to sing. I cringed. Dad has a really terrible singing voice—"if he is *the sunshine of my life.*"

"D'you get it?" Dad asked his students. "*Sunshine*—and he's my *son.*"

To my surprise, the students cracked up. I guess they have lower standards for humor up here. They also don't laugh the way kids do in the city. The noise Dad's students make is more like a twitter, and they cover their mouths when they do it. Like they feel bad for laughing.

That was when I started to understand why Dad likes it so much up here. It's not just the snow and the fresh air. No one in the civilized world could put up with his goofy jokes or his singing. Up here they thought he was funny.

Geraldine Snowflake is the first one to say anything when I walk into room 218. Geraldine's pretty in a way I'm not used to. She's nothing like Tammy Akerman at my school in Montreal. Tammy has blond wavy hair, and she wears tight T-shirts that drive me crazy.

Geraldine has long dark hair in a thick braid down her back. Her eyes are so dark they look like they're navy blue. She's wearing a baggy sweatshirt, though when she gets up to sharpen her pencil, I can tell she's got a nice body underneath it. Geraldine doesn't try to be pretty; she just is.

I cracked up when Dad mentioned over the phone how he had a student whose last name was Snowflake. "I laughed when I first heard it too," Dad said. "It's a translation from Inuktitut, and I guess the name stuck. Like snow."

Dad's the king of lame jokes. After he makes one, he actually waits for you to laugh. And if you don't, he says something like, "Don't think your old man is funny, hey?" Then of course I have to tell him how funny he is. What I don't say is I mean funny strange, not funny ha-ha.

Geraldine's dark eyes look worried when I walk past her desk. She's still watching me when I slip off my ski jacket. "What's wrong?" she wants to know.

I can feel the other kids' eyes on me too. "Where's your dad, anyhow?" Earl Etok asks. "He's never late." Earl has dark circles under his eyes and he's wearing khaki-colored cargo pants that hang so low on his hips they look like they're about to fall off.

Lenny Etok comes in after I do. He's a big guy with wide shoulders and a gut that spills out over the top of his jeans like a spare tire. There's something familiar-looking about him. "What's going on?" he wants to know.

"English teacher's late," Geraldine tells him, without looking up from her composition. They sure keep their sentences short up here.

I take a deep breath. My nerves are shot, and I'm afraid I might start to bawl. Then what'll they think of me? "His dog got hit by a truck," I manage to say. "I took her out for a run. That's when it happened." I pause to catch my breath. "We're supposed to work on our compositions till he gets here."

At first, no one says a word. Lenny sits down at his desk and reaches inside for a sheet of loose-leaf paper.

I shift from one foot to the other. Don't they have anything to say? Don't they want to know if Tarksalik's all right? And what am I supposed to do now? Work on some dumb composition and pretend everything's fine?

Lenny breaks the silence. "A run?" he asks, rolling his eyes. "Why would you go for a run in the middle of winter?"

It's the kind of question that doesn't need an answer. What Lenny really means is he thinks I'm stupid.

Earl looks up from his composition. "Who hit her?" he wants to know. His voice is totally flat, without any trace of emotion in it.

"I don't know. The guy just kept driving." I clench my fist under the desk. If the driver had stopped, we would've been able to get Tarksalik over to Mathilde's sooner, and Tarksalik wouldn't have had to drag herself to the side of the road. The thought of her doing that is almost worse than the memory of seeing her body fly up into the air.

The bit about the driver taking off gets Lenny and his friends a little more excited. Now they're all looking at me. "What color truck was it?" Lenny and Earl ask at the same time.

"Red. It was a red pickup truck."

"I bet it was Stanley from the airport. He's got a red pickup truck," Earl says. "Did he have straight black hair?"

I don't bother answering. Everyone up here has straight black hair.

No one asks about Tarksalik. Don't they want to know how she is? People wouldn't act like this in Montreal. Even if I told the story to a complete stranger—say, someone on the bus—he'd be concerned about the dog. Do I ever wish I were home!

In the end, it's Geraldine who finally mentions Tarksalik, only when she does, she doesn't sound too sympathetic. "Dog dead?" she asks, shrugging her shoulders. She makes it sound like it's no bigger deal than what we're having for lunch. My whole body tenses up. What's wrong with these people? Don't they have hearts?

"Tarksalik's not dead," I tell her, trying to sound as matter-of-fact as she does. "Mathilde doesn't think she broke any bones."

Lenny is slumped over on his desk. Something tells me he was up late, and probably not because he was working on his composition. He lifts his head, and when he speaks, the words come out slow and choppy. "If the dog's in pain, how come you guys didn't just shoot her?"

Lenny makes a gun with his fingers. Then he points it at the side of his head and pulls the trigger. His dark eyes shine like embers. The other kids twitter behind their hands.

At first, I don't say anything. I can't believe Lenny just said that or that the others think it's funny. Then again, they laughed at Dad's dumb joke yesterday. "You've got to be kidding," I say to Lenny.

Lenny doesn't bother to cover his mouth when he yawns. "I'm not kidding. I'm thinking of the dog." He leans into his chair and rocks on its back legs.

For a second, I feel like I'm going to be sick. Imagine suggesting we shoot Tarksalik! How can that be "thinking of the dog"?

"You shoulda shot her," Lenny mutters into his sleeve, but loud enough so I'll hear him. "Put her out of her pain."

It's the sneer that comes afterward that makes me realize why Lenny seems so familiar. Why didn't I see it before? Lenny reminds me of Roland Ipkins. The thought makes me feel even sicker.

The one good thing about coming up to no man's land was finally escaping Roland Ipkins, a first-class asshole, who, since grade two, has made tormenting me a personal hobby.

Only now it feels like I've just met Roland Ipkins's Inuit double.

And I thought this day couldn't get any worse.

THree

"All right, ladies and gents," Dad says, shaking the snow off his parka before hanging it over the back of his chair, "let's see what progress you've made on those compositions." Dad's voice sounds forced, and I can tell from the fine lines at the outside corners of his eyes that he's worried.

I want to know how Tarksalik is doing, but I can't ask in front of everyone. Especially not after what Lenny just said. Besides, Dad and I have this arrangement: for the next five months, I'm just another student in room 218. Students don't go asking their teachers personal questions in the middle of class.

I try catching Dad's eye, but he's already working his way around the circle of students, checking topic sentences and saying how important it is to find just the right words to express your thoughts. "There's no point saying 'very cold,'" I hear him tell Lenny, "if what you mean to say is 'freezing.'"

I can hear Lenny scratching out the words. "Okay, I get it," he says. "Freezing."

"Very good," Dad tells him.

Lenny nudges my dad and makes a loud guffawing sound. "Hey, Bill, you just said 'very'!"

It's weird hearing Dad's students call him Bill. Dad only has eight students—nine, if you count me—and the atmosphere in room 218 is way more relaxed than in any classroom I've ever been in. Dad's class is a mix of grades ten and eleven. "The reason my group is so small," Dad had explained over dinner last night, "is because many kids in George River drop out by grade ten."

"By grade ten?" Most kids I know in Montreal at least finish high school.

"What do they do all day?" I asked, looking out the window and seeing nothing except a lot of snow and a few houses with satellite dishes.

"Some of them go hunting or fishing. But most of them stay home and watch TV. Too many of them drink and do drugs," Dad said, shaking his head. "The ones in my class are the cream of the crop." Dad looked up at me. "I'm lucky to be their teacher. They're good kids. Decent kids."

Lenny's head is back on his desk, and now he's started to snore. The sound reminds me of an old radiator. It's hard to think of Lenny as the cream of anybody's crop. I expect Dad to say something, but when he passes Lenny's spot, all Dad does is pat Lenny's shoulder.

Small classes are one of the things that attracted Dad to the North. But Mom says it wasn't just that. "Your father's always had a restless soul—all that traveling he used to do. He's always looking for the next adventure," she told me. "It's one of the reasons we didn't last. I'm the sort of person who likes to stay in one place. I think you're a mix of the two of us. You know, Noah, you might end up enjoying this adventure more than you expect to."

If it weren't for Roland Ipkins, I'd have been perfectly happy staying in Montreal and having Dad visit at Christmas and for a few weeks in the summer. Mom's the one who pushed me to come up here. I think she was looking forward to having the house to herself. Not that she ever said so, but I got the feeling. What she did say was that she thought it was important for a guy my age to know his father. "You're a young man now, and you need a role model. Even if your dad and I didn't get along, he's a good man. And it's high time you got to know him better."

Which is how she talked me into doing a school term in George River. Of course, now that I'm here, I realize what a huge mistake it was. I don't fit in, and so far all I've done is cause trouble. If it weren't for me, Tarksalik would be running around outside, happy and healthy. I should never have let Mom talk me into coming up here.

It isn't till Dad gets to my side of the circle that I finally get to ask about Tarksalik. "How's she doing?" I whisper. Then I ask the question I've been thinking ever since I left Mathilde's house. "Do you think she's gonna make it?"

Dad sucks in his breath. I suck mine in too. I don't think I'll be able to live with myself if Tarksalik dies. When he speaks, Dad's voice is really low. I can tell he doesn't want the others to hear. Maybe he knows how they feel about injured animals. "I hope so, Son," he says. "I sure hope so."

I can feel my chest tighten. Tarksalik's not out of the woods yet. I remember what Mathilde said about the first few hours being critical. Does that mean if Tarksalik makes it through today, she'll be okay? And will she ever be able to run again? For a second, I remember how she looked running on the tundra with the early morning sun shining on her. She looked like she was made to run.

It's only when I am standing at the lockers, putting on my coat before recess, that I realize Dad didn't ask how *I* was doing. What happened to Tarksalik is horrible, but hey, I'm in pretty rough shape too. And he is my dad, isn't he?

It's a short walk from the school to Dad's apartment. I could take the road, but there's a path that's quicker and goes right by Dad's back door. There are huge snowdrifts on either side of the path, and the wind is picking up. I can see the town straight ahead. The satellite dishes look like flying saucers against the pale blue sky. TV, I figure, is one way people can escape this place. Can't say I blame them.

There's one huge satellite dish mounted on a tall metal tower in the center of town. That's the dish that lets people here have Internet access.

Outside a small bungalow, I spot something hanging on a clothesline. At first, I think it's a pair of jeans. Why would anyone hang jeans outside in the dead of winter? It's not as if they're going to dry out here. But as I get closer, I realize it's not jeans; it's a sealskin pelt. Seeing the pelt reminds me again how far I am from Montreal.

Earl Etok is walking with me, which isn't the same as us walking together. He was behind me when we left school, and since he's more used to trudging through heavy snow than I am, he's caught up with me.

I hear the loud *click-click* of a truck shifting into reverse. At first, the noise startles me. I'm a little skittish around trucks today. But when I look out toward the street, I see it isn't a pickup truck. It's way bigger and it's got a huge yellow cylinder on the back. There's writing under the driver's window, but because it's in Inuktitut, all I see are a bunch of weird lines and squiggles.

When Earl waves at the driver, he waves back.

"That's my *ataata*," Earl tells me. "I mean my dad," he adds, once he realizes I have no idea what he's talking about. From the way he says it, I get the feeling Earl is proud of his *ataata* for driving what must be the biggest truck in town. It's a weird beginning to a conversation, but hey, who am I to complain? I'm glad for the company.

"Cool truck," I say. The truck has pulled up alongside Dad's apartment, and now Earl's dad is jumping down from the cab. He's wearing heavy work gloves, and his parka has dark streaks on it. He attaches a long thick hose to a metal box on the side of the building. The equipment makes sucking sounds.

It's only when Earl's dad is nearly done that I notice the awful stench. It's worse than anything I've ever smelled, and the cold air is making the smell even stronger. I can taste the stink at the back of my throat.

"Very cool truck," Earl says. He seems oblivious to the odor. "My *ataata*'s got a real good job. One of the best jobs in George River. Pays real well, I'll tell you that."

By then, I've figured out what the Inuktitut words on Earl's dad's truck must say: *Kangiqsualujjuaq Sewage Department*. There's no citywide plumbing system up here; the thick layer of permafrost means underground pipes would freeze. Every house must have its own septic tank, and someone has to empty those tanks. That someone is Earl's dad.

I can't help thinking how in Montreal, a kid probably wouldn't boast about how his dad collects shit. "That's great," I say, trying to sound like I mean it. I don't ask whether Mr. Etok gets danger pay because of his exposure to some pretty toxic fumes.

"Sure is," Earl says, grinning. "My *ataata*'s a good guy. He shows up for work real reliable, five days a week. And when I'm done school, he says he's gonna try to get me a job on the truck too."

Dad is home before me. He, Mathilde and Steve have already brought Tarksalik back to the apartment, and she's sprawled on a blanket in front of the TV. Usually she lifts her head or barks when someone comes to the door, but she doesn't do either of those things when I let myself in. At least, I tell myself, she's still alive. That's something, anyway.

"It's probably the medication," Dad says, watching her from his corduroy armchair. "She's pretty zonked out."

I help Dad tear open some green garbage bags and spread them out under Tarksalik's blanket. It's tricky, because we don't want her to move. We try our best to get the garbage bags under where her rump is. That way she won't soak through the carpet if she has to pee.

"Listen," Dad says, "there's a storytelling event at the community center tonight. I don't want to leave Tarksalik alone. Not tonight. But you should go, Noah. The Inuit, especially the elders, are wonderful storytellers. You'll have a good time. Besides, it's a way for you to learn a little about George River and the people who live here."

That's another thing that's always bugged me about Dad. Even when I was little and he still lived with us, he had this way of turning everything into a learning opportunity. Doesn't he ever quit being a teacher?

But in the end, I don't object to going to the talk at the community center. Some old coot is going to be telling an Inuit legend. I tell Dad how eager I am to learn about Inuit culture.

Dad laps that up. "I know George River may not seem like much at first, Noah, but it's a fascinating place. And the people who live here, well, they're deep. Deeper than a lot of people I know from the city. I'm really glad you're open to this new experience."

That's all bull. I'm not open. No way. What I am is trapped in this frozen hellhole for the next five months. I'm about as interested in Inuit culture as I am in collecting rare stamps. But, truth is, with Tarksalik lying zonked out on her blanket, Dad hovering over her and the whole apartment beginning to reek of dog pee, I can't wait to get out of here. Even if it means listening to some lame old legend.

Four

I can tell Dad is really upset about the dog, because he hasn't checked the temperature since I left for my run this morning. But I don't need a computer to tell me it's way friggin' colder here at night than during the day. The air is so cold it bites. If I hurry, I figure I can make it to the community center in about five minutes. One good thing about George River is that nothing's very far away. Back home, I have to take the bus or métro to get anyplace.

A couple of dogs bark when I pass them. They've got bent-back ears and the same black, brown and white coloring as Tarksalik. When one bares his teeth, I back away. The dogs don't seem to belong to anyone; something tells me they haven't had their rabies shots. I think about Tarksalik and how she used to be like them, fending for herself in the cold and living on scraps. Grateful, Dad called her. Only now that I let her get hit by a truck, she's probably not so grateful anymore. She'd have been better off out here with these drooling mongrels.

I can't say I'm looking forward to my night out. If this were Montreal, I might be able to score tickets to a Habs game at the Bell Centre. Chris L'Ecuyer's dad has season's tickets, and sometimes he lets us have them. Or I could meet Chris at the Second Cup in our neighborhood and we could pretend to do homework while we check out hot girls. Right now, though, my life in Montreal feels like it never really happened.

Besides the school, the community center is the biggest building in George River. It has these enormous glass windows that look out over the river. Like everything else in town, the community center looks new. New buildings don't do much for me. For one thing, the houses in George River all look pretty much the same. They have aluminum siding, small square windows and little closed-in porches out front. They look like someone without much imagination dropped them from the sky.

Where Mom and I live in Montreal, most of the houses are at least a hundred years old and the neighborhood feels like it has history. Not to mention trees. Big old trees that in summer make a canopy over our street and in winter get blanketed by snow. I never realized how cool trees were until I got here and there weren't any.

Dad told me tonight's talk is in the upstairs meeting room. It looks like there's a No Boots rule here too. I park mine in the front hallway. I pass a kitchen on the ground floor. When I peek in, I see a couple of Inuit ladies laying cookies out on a tray. Though I've never met her before, one of them waves when she sees me. "Ay!" she says. I've noticed that's the Inuit way of saying hello. I wave back. Maybe I'll get my hands on some of those cookies later.

Upstairs, a few people are sitting on metal folding chairs, but most are squatting on the floor, their legs tucked underneath them. Man, that looks uncomfortable! In Montreal, people would be scrambling for the chairs. But here it works the other way around; the Inuit seem to think squatting on the floor is the better option.

Rhoda, Steve's wife, is sitting on a folding chair. Celia is with her. Rhoda waves me over. She's saved me a place on her other side. Dad must have let her know I'd be coming. "How ya' doin', Noah?" she asks when I sit down. I can feel her watching my face. Celia is peeking at me too.

"Tarksalik's not so good."

"I heard," Rhoda says, "but what about *you*?"

It's the first time all day anyone has asked how I'm doing, and I feel my throat tighten. It's been an awful day. "I can't stop picturing the accident," I tell her.

"Poor you," she says, rumpling my hair the way my mom sometimes does. Then Rhoda looks straight at me. Her dark eyes look kind. "Replaying the accident in your mind is perfectly normal, Noah. You're having what's called a post–traumatic stress reaction." She says those last words slowly, as if she wants me to realize she's just said something important. "It's perfectly understandable. You just have to remember one thing: what happened to Tarksalik wasn't your fault."

I try to smile, but I can't. My lips feel frozen. "If only I hadn't taken Tarksalik out with me. If only I'd kept her closer. If only I hadn't gone for a run in the first place," I mutter. The thoughts have been hovering in my mind all day, and now, saying the words out loud makes me feel even worse. If only.

Rhoda looks me in the eye. "It wasn't your fault," she says again.

If only I could believe her.

The guy who's talking tonight is one of the elders in the community. In his case the word "elder" is an understatement. He looks like he's about 200. He's got stooped shoulders, and his face is so wrinkled his skin looks like it's made out of tissue paper. I guess he never heard of sunblock. The only thing not so ancient-looking about him is his hair: it's still mostly black, with wiry gray streaks.

The guy's name is Charlie. Charlie Etok. Why are half the people in this town named Etok?

I spot Lenny in the audience, sitting at the back with a couple of guys I don't recognize. They're probably some of the local dropouts. At least Lenny's awake. He nudges one of his friends when he catches me looking in their direction. Again, I can't help thinking of Roland Ipkins. He's got a gang of henchmen too. I look away as fast as I can.

Someone dims all the lights, except for one spotlight that's shining on Charlie. He clears his throat, and then he clears it a second time. "Tonight," he says in a voice that is surprisingly strong for such an old guy, "I'm going to tell you a legend my *ataata* and his *ataata* told me." He stops to take a rest. If this is how the guy tells stories, stopping for a nap after every sentence, it's gonna be one long night.

"This legend is about a couple of kids, a spirit and a dog team."

My back stiffens. I've had enough of dogs for one day, thank you very much. I consider getting up and going to the bathroom so I can skip this part of the legend, but Rhoda pats my hand. It's just a story, I tell myself, and with the lights so dim, maybe I'll be able to catch a few z's. Isn't that what Inuit legends are for?

People have been talking, but now that Charlie has started, the room is quiet, except for a black-haired baby wailing in the front row. The baby is sitting inside a pouch on the back of his mom's parka, but now she lifts him out and settles him on her lap. I've never seen so much hair on a baby. Charlie grins. Let me guess: that kid must be another member of the Etok clan.

I fidget in my chair. The guy hasn't even started telling his grampa's legend, and already I'm restless. I cross and uncross my legs, but it doesn't help.

"We didn't always live in towns like this one," Charlie says. He lifts his chin to the big windows. Not only does he talk really slowly, but his voice doesn't go up and down the way I'm used to.

"No, we Inuit never used to stay in one place too long," Charlie continues. From the way he says it, I can tell he thinks moving around like that was a good thing. I remember what my mom said about Dad having a restless soul.

No wonder he gets along so well with the Inuit. But when I think about how cold it is outside, I'm glad not to be some nomad spending the night in an igloo. Charlie must be a pretty tough old guy.

"The *Qallunaat*—the white men—made us settle in one town," Charlie says. For a second, his eyes land on me. I scan the room. I don't know why I didn't realize it before, but I'm the only white person here. It's not a feeling I'm used to.

Part of me wants to call out, "Hey, don't go blaming me for what some white guys did before I was even born." On the other hand, what Charlie just said is pretty interesting. It helps explain why so many of the buildings in George River—the community center, the houses, the medical clinic and the school—look new. The Inuit were nomads until white men showed up here. And even if I wasn't born when all that happened, there's no denying I am a white man.

Charlie's droning on again. I sure wish he'd hurry up and get the legend over with. "We used to follow the caribou and hunt for seal, setting up camp along the way."

Charlie closes his eyes and smiles. I figure he's remembering those days. I sure hope he was wearing a warm parka. "Tonight," he says, "I'm going to tell you the legend of Kajutaijug."

Kajutaijug? What kind of weird name is that?

There is a low moan from the people sitting at the front. They seem to know the legend. Judging from their reaction, I figure it's a scary story. On the other hand, what do these people know? They don't even have a movie theater in George River. I bet most of them have never even seen the first *Halloween* movie. Still, with any luck, maybe the old guy's story will take my mind off Tarksalik and the rest of my troubles.

Charlie takes a deep breath. "One time, a long, long time ago, our people were preparing to move to a new camp. It was the end of winter so the days were getting longer. We had to pack everything up, and of course, in those days, we traveled everywhere by dogsled. Let me tell you," Charlie says, looking up at us, "our sled dogs were something. Even in the worst snowstorm, they could find their way better than any GPS system ever invented."

Some people at the front of the room laugh. Even if they don't own cars, they all know about GPS systems. Maybe they *have* seen *Halloween*.

"And those dogs were strong too. They were bred for pulling. A team of sled dogs could pull hundreds and hundreds of pounds. They could pull five caribou carcasses or a polar bear."

This legend is going to take forever—and then some—to tell. I wish I could stretch my legs, but there isn't any room.

Charlie is still yakking away. I think he likes the attention. "But there was so much to bring when they moved that time, even the sled dogs couldn't manage everything in one trip. So the elders had to leave a group of people behind. 'Don't worry,' the elders told those people. 'We'll be back soon. We promise. Just wait for us here, okay?'"

Charlie looks up at the audience, and I can tell he wants us to feel like he's one of those elders and we're the people he's leaving behind. It's not working for me. All I can think about is how bored I am. I don't see the point of telling legends.

"Two days went by, then three days, then four." Charlie's getting tense. I can tell because he's finally speeding up. Thank god for that. Maybe I'll score a couple of those cookies in the next half century.

"The people that were left behind got tired of waiting. They were hungry too. They ate up all the provisions." That gets me wondering some more about those cookies. Were any of them chocolate? I'll eat chocolate anything. "The seal meat and the caribou. They shot some ptarmigan—"

"Ptarmigan?" Without meaning to, I say the word out loud.

A woman in the front row turns and shushes me.

"Sorry," I whisper.

Celia leans over her mom to poke my arm. Once she has my attention, Celia bends her elbows and flaps her arms. A ptarmigan must be a bird.

"Thanks," I whisper to Celia.

"—but a few ptarmigan weren't enough to fill their empty bellies. So on the fifth day, a boy and a girl"—I notice Charlie's eyes land on Lenny and his friends—"kids about your age—well, they started heading for the new camp. On foot." I can tell from the way Charlie is shaking his head he doesn't think that was a very wise move.

A small girl sitting on the floor groans. "What did their *anaana* and *ataata* say?" she calls out.

Charlie shrugs. "You know how young folks are. Those two kids wouldn't listen to anybody, least of all their *anaana* and *ataata*. The two of them just headed out into the snow, following the tracks the dogsleds had made five days before. After they'd been walking for two or three hours, the snow came. At first, it was just light flakes, but then the sky grew purplish black and a storm—a fierce one—blew in. The tracks got covered in no time." Charlie pauses, and when he starts to speak again, his voice is so low it isn't much louder than a whisper. "And then, they heard a terrible sound."

One of the grownups actually whimpers. Sheesh, I think, what's wrong with you? It's just a story.

"The sound those kids heard," Charlie continues, "was louder than a scream, deeper than a moan and higher pitched than a dog's bark. It was the worst sound they ever heard, so they covered their ears." Charlie covers his ears now too, then bends over a little as if that might also help protect him from the sound he's describing. "But the sound went right through their mittens and their *nassaks*."

This time Rhoda translates. She taps the black and red wool cap on her lap.

Nassak. I nod and mouth the word so the woman in the front row won't give me the evil eye again.

Charlie picks up even more speed now that he's finally come to the climax of his story. I hope the old guy won't have a heart attack. This is probably the most excitement he's had in, like, 150 years.

"The boy saw Kajutaijug first. He wanted to warn the girl, but he was too frightened to speak, so he just pointed." Charlie lifts one hand and points a wrinkly finger at the audience. "There—right in front of them, not more than a couple of feet away—was Kajutaijug."

There's another moan from the audience. Louder this time. I remember Dad telling me about something called "the willing suspension of disbelief." Basically, that means people who listen to stories or read them or watch them on TV or in a movie, have to buy in; they have to believe the story could be true. Well, Charlie's audience is suspending their disbelief all right.

But not me. I don't believe in spirits, especially ones with hard-to-pronounce names.

"Kajutaijug had no body." This story is getting weirder by the second. "She was just an enormous head on top of two feet. And those feet were big, as big as tree stumps. And her face, oh Lord, what an ugly face she had! The ugliest face those two kids ever saw. And Kajutaijug had a breast growing from each cheek." That part of Charlie's description makes some people in the audience—even me—laugh.

"I guess Kajutaijug couldn't get a job for the Playboy channel," I hear Lenny whisper to his friends.

Charlie doesn't seem to mind the interruptions, or that Lenny just mentioned the Playboy channel. I'll bet Charlie doesn't even know what the Playboy channel is.

Still, he slaps his thigh. "You're right about that, Lenny," he says, grinning. "Breasts are nice"—that makes us laugh again—"but not when they grow where cheeks should be."

"Gross! That'd be s-so gross," one of Lenny's pals calls out. The way he slurs his words makes me wonder if he's been drinking. It's illegal to buy or sell alcohol in George River. The law is supposed to eliminate alcoholism, but Dad told me how people get around it by buying bootleg liquor or ordering it up from the south.

Charlie clears his throat. I can tell he wants to get back to his story. "And when Kajutaijug walked, dragging one foot-stump after the other, she made those terrible noises again. Only louder. The whole tundra shook from the sound of her. Even the river and the sky shook."

It's so dark outside now that we can't see the point where the river meets the sky. The only light is coming from a few houses near the shore and from the smattering of stars in the sky.

"Did Kajutaijug eat them up?" the little girl calls out.

Charlie wags his finger. "Hold on," he says, "I'm not at that part yet."

Rhoda leans forward onto the edge of her chair. I can't believe she is suspending her disbelief too.

But I guess for a made-up story, this one isn't all bad. It's got suspense, at least, and I'm starting to like the sound of Charlie's voice.

"The children tried running away from Kajutaijug, but she was too fast for them, even on those stumpy legs of hers. Besides, by then the kids were tired and hungry and afraid.

Charlie looks up at the audience. "Fear can tire a person out worse than anything else."

"Kajutaijug opened her mouth—it looked like a cave inside there—and licked her lips. She used her long tongue to scoop those two kids up from the snow. Then, just as she was about to gobble them up, she heard something. At first, the sound was low, like a rumble, but it got louder. And it frightened Kajutaijug."

The little girl laughs and then covers her mouth. She likes the idea of something frightening Kajutaijug. Other people start laughing too.

"It was the sled dogs. They came back for the Inuit who were left behind. Just in time too. Those dogs bit the fat ankles on Kajutaijug's stumps. Kajutaijug cried out in pain, and when she did, the children fell out of her mouth and back onto the snow. When they turned around, Kajutaijug was gone. Vanished into the frozen night."

Charlie bows his head. Suddenly, he looks very old again.

"It's a good story," someone calls out. Someone else claps, and then others start clapping too. Lenny and his friends put their fingers in their mouths and whistle.

I clap too. Not just to be polite, but also because I'm looking at Charlie's lined skin and black hair and thinking about what a tough life he's had, how he's lived on the land and hunted for his food. And I'm looking at all the other people in the room lining up to thank Charlie and clap him on the shoulder. You'd think he'd just given them a present, which I guess, in a way, he did. If you don't mind stories for presents.

Through the window, the stars seem to have grown brighter. As Rhoda, Celia and I get up from our chairs, there is a loud boom outside. So loud it makes the windows rattle.

"It's just thunder," a woman says.

The little girl doesn't believe her. "It's not thunder," she says, planting her thumb in her mouth. "It's Kajutaijug."

I think of telling the girl there's no such thing as Kajutaijug. But then the lady from downstairs appears with her tray of cookies. I think I smell chocolate.

FIVE

When I get back, Dad is asleep in his armchair. The TV is off, but he's still clutching the remote in one hand. There's a pile of compositions and a red pen on the floor next to him.

Tarksalik is lying on her bed of blankets and green garbage bags. Her head is extended between her forelegs. The light from a streetlamp makes the pale spot on her forehead glow. Though she seems to be asleep, she makes a groaning sound when I come in. Even from where I'm standing in the hallway, I notice how the fur around her belly and hind legs looks matted. Must be from all the dried blood. Guess it'll be a while before she can have a proper bath.

Poor girl. And for what must be the hundredth time today, I replay the morning in my head—only now I try changing the order of things.

"How 'bout I take the dog out with me on my run?" I ask Dad, who is opening the curtains and going on about the beauty of the landscape.

Only this time, Dad says no. "I'll take her myself, Son. I can use the fresh air. Go enjoy your run. Just be careful. I was just checking the weather online and you'll never believe..."

Of course, that wasn't how things went.

I tiptoe down the hallway to the bathroom. The only noise in the house is the steady hum of Dad's freezer. Dad has an unnatural attachment to his freezer, which he paid a lot of money to have shipped up from Montreal last summer. The first thing he did when I arrived was show me all the stuff he's got stocked in there: chicken breasts and steaks and frozen mini pizzas and *tourtières*.

"And two dozen containers of my homemade spaghetti sauce," he said proudly. You'd think he was a pirate showing off his treasure chest and that those frozen dinners were gold bars. "I try to cook ahead on weekends. I've got enough food in here to last all winter. Or nearly."

Thinking back on that conversation reminds me of the legend of Kajutaijug. It must've been scary for the people who were left behind to realize they were out of food. In all my life, I've never once had to worry about going hungry. All I ever had to do in Montreal was open the fridge. If there wasn't anything I felt like eating, I'd write down what I wanted, and Mom would pick it up for me the next time she was at the grocery store, which was just about every single day.

I reach for the dental floss. Mom made me promise to floss every night. I watch my reflection in the mirror as I slide the floss between my front teeth. Something about my eyes makes me look older than fifteen. Then again, it's been an awful day, and I need sleep. But I have a feeling I won't be getting much of that tonight. Not if those pictures of the accident keep looping around in my head, like the road in town that goes from the gas station to the dump and back again.

"Don't let Tarksalik die," I whisper. It isn't exactly a prayer, but kind of. I don't press my palms together or go down on my knees, but if I thought that would help, I'd do it. Still, I hope somebody—somewhere—is listening.

I don't hear Dad get up, so I'm startled when I see his reflection behind mine in the mirror. We have the same brown curly hair, only I've got more of it. I wonder if thirty years from now, I'll be going bald at the top too. I hope not.

Dad rubs his forehead. I can tell he's only half-awake. "How was the talk?"

"Pretty cool." I figure that's what he wants to hear.

"Everything's pretty cool in George River. In fact, it's minus forty-two tonight."

I try to laugh. Dad must be feeling better if he's been back on the weather website. "How's Tarksalik?" I ask.

Dad stretches his arms out behind him and sighs. "I can't tell for sure. But I'm going to the store for a box of diapers. In case...you know..."

I put the dental floss back on the shelf next to Dad's shaving cream. "No," I say, "I'll go."

I've only been back in Dad's apartment for five minutes and already I can't wait to leave. At least, I tell myself when I open the front door and a gust of minus forty-two degree wind practically knocks me over, I'm doing something and not just sitting around, feeling lousy.

George River only has two stores: the Co-op, which is owned by the Inuit community, and the Northern, which used to be part of the Hudson's Bay Company. The Co-op closes at six, but the Northern stays open later. Luckily, it's only a few doors over from Dad's. January nights in Montreal can get pretty cold, but they're balmy compared to what the cold feels like up here. It isn't just the temperature; it's the dry air and maybe, too, the feeling that I'm hundreds and hundreds of kilometers away from a real city. I pull up the collar of my jacket so it covers my chin.

A snowmobile roars by, followed by two others. I wonder where they're all off to at this time of night. One of the drivers waves in my direction, and I wave back.

A fourth snowmobile stops to let me cross the street. The driver looks like he's in his twenties. A girl his age is sitting behind him, her hands clasped around his waist. "Where you headed?" I ask them.

"Over to the dump," the guy says.

"No place," his girlfriend adds.

I guess driving round in circles beats hanging out at home, watching TV or listening to their grandparents tell legends.

There aren't too many places in George River for teenagers to hang out, especially at night. I'm not surprised to see a couple of guys smoking in the narrow hallway leading into the Northern. They stop talking when I squeeze past them. I can feel them watching me, checking out my ski jacket and ski gloves, so different from their fur-trimmed parkas and caribou-skin mittens. I get the same feeling I had at the community center. I'm the only white guy here too. I wonder if Dad feels the same way when he goes out or whether he's stopped noticing.

One of the guys burps, and I smell beer. Definitely beer. Dad says some Inuit don't hold their alcohol too well. Of course, it was white people who brought alcohol to the North in the first place. I guess it's one more problem we're responsible for.

"Who's he?" I hear one of the guys whisper as I step inside the store.

Word must spread quickly in a town of only 700 people, because someone else answers. "His dad's a teacher at the school. You know that guy Bill?"

I consider saying "Hi," but I decide that'd be too awkward. Instead I lift my hand and wave it behind my head as I pass them.

"Have a good night," one of the guys calls out.

That takes me by surprise. In Montreal, some guy my age who I didn't know would never wish me a good night. More likely, he'd ignore me, or maybe say something rude. I slow down for a second. "You too," I tell the guy.

It takes a few seconds for my eyes to adjust to the fluorescent lighting inside the Northern. "Hey, Noah," a voice calls from behind the cash register. I look up and see Geraldine. I guess I shouldn't be surprised that in a town as small as this one, I'd actually know someone. Still, it's nice to hear her call my name. It makes me feel like I'm part of something.

Geraldine's resting her elbows on the counter. "You work here?" I ask her.

"What does it look like?"

"It looks like you work here."

Geraldine grins. Her black hair gleams under the harsh lights. "Every day after school and all day Saturday."

"Cool," I say, mainly because I can't think of what else to say, and I really don't want to ask her what aisle diapers are in.

The store carries mostly dry goods like cereal, soup and pasta, frozen foods and soft drinks. There's a whole aisle of Coke bottles, but only half an aisle of fresh fruits and vegetables. Some of them look like they've been sitting around since the Paleolithic era. I notice broccoli that has gone yellowish brown at the tips and carrots with fuzzy white spots. Gross.

"It's not a good day for produce," Geraldine calls from the front of the store. "Fruits and vegetables get flown in tomorrow. You better wait till then if you want to make a salad."

"Thanks for the tip," I call back.

Because grocery prices are so high in Nunavik, Dad e-mailed me a two-page shopping list of stuff he wanted me to bring up: ten dozen Montreal bagels, hamburger meat and boneless chicken thighs, oranges, apples and grapefruits, toothpaste and shampoo. And eight cases of beer.

I find the diapers in the last aisle. "They're for Tarksalik," I tell Geraldine when I get to the cash.

"Uh-huh," she says as she rings up the diapers. From the sounds of it, you'd think Geraldine was used to people buying diapers for their dogs.

"She's not doing too well," I say. Geraldine hasn't asked about Tarksalik, but I feel like I need to talk to somebody about everything that's happened, and right now she's my only option.

"Uh-huh," Geraldine says again.

I have a feeling I'm not going to get a lot of sympathy from her. Maybe she also thinks we should have shot Tarksalik to put her out of her misery. "See you tomorrow," I say, tucking the bag of diapers under my arm and zipping up my coat.

Geraldine touches my elbow. "Did you go to the talk at the community center?" she asks.

"Uh-huh." I'm starting to sound like an Inuk.

"I wish I could've gone, but I had to work," Geraldine says. "I'm saving up to buy my nephew something nice for his birthday."

"You've got a nephew?"

"Uh-huh. Jeremiah. He lives with us. So what did you think of our community center?"

"I liked it." It's not a very cool thing to say to a pretty girl, but I can't think of anything else. And now it's as if I can't stop talking. "You get a great view of the river from those windows. Your school's nice too. Every school I ever went to in Montreal was, like, a hundred years old.

You guys are lucky to have a new school. Usually I like old buildings, but not when it comes to schools."

I expect Geraldine to say "uh-huh" again, but this time she doesn't. "Did you hear what happened to our old school?" she asks, dropping her voice.

"Nope. What happened?"

"It got destroyed. In an avalanche. New Year's Eve 1999. We were having a New Year's Eve celebration there. Nine people died." Geraldine looks right at me. "Including my little cousin. He was only two. We tried and tried, but we couldn't pull him out from under the snow. My sister named her boy after him." Geraldine takes a deep breath. I can tell she's not used to saying so much all at once.

I shiver, and it isn't because of the cold air that blows in when another customer enters the store. "I'm sorry," I tell her. "I had no idea. And I'm sorry about your cousin. That must have been awful."

If I can't forget what happened to Tarksalik, how does Geraldine forget trying to pull her little cousin out from under the snow? I wish I could ask her how she does it. How she manages to keep going to school and working at the Northern even after all that.

Geraldine reaches for a bottle of spray cleaner. She sprays the counter and then dries it with a sheet of paper towel before she looks back up at me. The air around us smells like ammonia. "Accidents are part of life," she says. "Death too."

45

SIX

Dad isn't getting much sleep. I know, because I'm awake too, lying in bed and replaying the accident over and over again in my head. It doesn't help that I can still hear kids *vrooming* by in their snowmobiles. Dad shuffles to the living room, talking in a low voice to Tarksalik. "It's okay, girl. I know it hurts. Sure it hurts."

I must doze off at some point, because the smell of coffee and the *blub-blub* sound of the percolator wake me up. I stumble out of bed. Mathilde is at Dad's door. She brings the cold air from outside with her into the apartment. She rubs her hands together to warm them up. Her fingers are red and chapped-looking.

"I know I'm early," she says, "but I've got to be at the clinic by seven thirty and I wanted to have a look at our girl first." She pets Tarksalik behind the ears. "How are you, *ma belle?*" she asks the dog, looking into her eyes as if she's expecting an answer.

Dad is busy pouring Mathilde a cup of coffee. "Milk, no sugar, coming up," he says. I figure Mathilde must come over for coffee a lot. How else would Dad know she doesn't take sugar? I take a better look at Mathilde. She's not bad looking, a bit pudgy, but she's got nice hazel eyes, and she's obviously good with animals. Then I look over at Dad. He's handing her a mug, and for a second their hands touch. Could the two of them be having a thing? I decide it's a definite possibility. But if I'm right, why hasn't Dad told me about it? It's not like I'd mind.

Tarksalik has arranged herself so we can't see her wound. But that doesn't stop Mathilde. She gulps down some coffee, then reaches over and lifts up one of Tarksalik's hind legs. Tarksalik makes a low moaning sound. "Careful," I say, "she bit me yesterday."

"You didn't tell me that," Dad calls from the kitchen, where he's gone to make toast.

Mathilde looks up at me. "Did she break the skin?"

"Nah," I say, "not really." I show her my hand. It's still a little sore.

Mathilde examines my hand. "She did break the skin. But it looks okay. Did you rinse it out and put on some antibiotic cream?"

"Uh-huh."

"Be glad it wasn't a person who bit you. Germs tend to be species specific, you know. Human bites can be a lot more dangerous than dog bites."

"I guess I had it coming," I mutter under my breath.

Mathilde pats the outside of my hand. Then she turns

back to check Tarksalik's eyes. "Her pupils don't seem to be dilated," she says. "I don't think there's any intracranial bleeding."

Mathilde gets up from where she's been kneeling on the floor and claps her hands like she's a kindergarten teacher letting us know playtime is over. "*Eh bien!* Tarksalik needs some exercise. Let's get this girl outside!"

Dad is juggling three plates of brown toast. His jaw drops. "Exercise?" he says. "You've got to be kidding. What this dog needs now is rest."

Mathilde puts her hands on her hips. I can tell right away she's upset. "Who's the nurse?" she asks Dad. "Me or you?"

Dad grimaces. "It's true I'm not the nurse. But my instincts tell me Tarksalik's not ready to go outside. Not yet, anyhow."

My instincts feel a lot like Dad's. Maybe it's genetic. Anyway, Tarksalik looks like she's been run over by a truck. Which, in her case, she has. "Don't you think maybe we should wait a while before we drag her outside?" I ask.

Mathilde glares at Dad and me. When she speaks, I can tell she's making a big effort not to lose her temper. "If you two insist on treating this dog like an invalid, she's going to stay an invalid. I spent most of my career working with orthopedic patients. I made them take a few steps the day after they had surgery on their knees or hips. They didn't always like me. Some of them swore at me. But I'll tell you something: they thanked me for it afterward. Each and every one of them."

Dad sighs and gives Mathilde a nervous smile. "Okay, then," he says. "I see your point."

Dad doesn't usually give in so easily. Maybe they *are* having a thing.

I'm still not sure dragging Tarksalik outside is the best idea though.

Mathilde tries to get Tarksalik to stand, but the poor dog just collapses back on her blanket. When Tarksalik looks up at Dad and me, it's as if she's trying to say, "Would you please get that woman to quit torturing me?"

Dad must be picking up the same message, because he turns to Mathilde and says, "Maybe we could try again tomorrow."

Mathilde ignores him. "Let's carry her outside," she says, directing Dad and me to each take an end of the blanket. Together, the three of us carry Tarksalik down the hallway, then down the steps and into the front yard. It's not an easy job with the poor dog wobbling in the middle of the blanket.

When we finally get her settled, Tarksalik's nose twitches in the cold, but that's the only part of her body that moves. Was it only yesterday I took her out for a run?

The sun is just beginning to rise over the George River, making the sky a purply orange. "Come on, Tarksalik," Mathilde says, tugging on the scruff of the dog's neck.

Tarksalik whimpers.

"Ouch," Dad says, wincing as if he's the one who was run over by a truck.

I know how Dad feels. For me, the worst part is looking into Tarksalik's eyes. They still have that milky, glazed-over look they had after the accident.

Tarksalik whimpers again. Mathilde has no sympathy. She tugs even harder on Tarksalik's neck. This time, I'm the one who says ouch.

Mathilde gives me a scowl.

Then, just like that, Tarksalik stands up on all four legs. "Tarksalik!" we say, all of us calling out her name at the same time. For a moment, the heaviness I've been carrying with me like a suitcase since yesterday morning lifts. Surely this means Tarksalik will be able to walk—and run—again.

But then, just as suddenly as Tarksalik got up, she drops back down on the blanket, landing with a heavy thud. She didn't even manage to stay up for three seconds. How is she ever going to run again?

Mathilde is not discouraged. "Good work!" she calls out. "Beautiful dog! Smart dog! Wonderful dog!" I notice Mathilde looks prettier when she's not being so bossy.

Tarksalik's tail shifts a little on the blanket. I get the feeling if she had more strength, she'd wag it. I guess even dogs like compliments.

"Up you go, Tarksalik!" Mathilde insists, tugging again on the scruff of the dog's neck.

This time, Tarksalik refuses to budge. And when Mathilde tries again, Tarksalik makes a low growl and bares her fangs. I back away from the blanket.

"I told you she isn't ready yet," Dad mutters.

Mathilde glares at Dad.

"Okay, okay," he says. "You're the boss."

Down the road, a snowmobile makes a chugging sound. A minute or so later, it pulls up in front of Dad's place. The driver is so bundled up inside his parka I can't see his face.

Whoever it is turns off the engine but doesn't get off the snowmobile. He just sits there, shaking his head while he watches Tarksalik and us. Though the stranger hasn't said anything, I can feel his disapproval. The dog is still refusing to stand up.

"Joseph!" Dad says, getting up from the snow and heading for the snowmobile. "I guess you heard about what happened to Tarksalik."

The man named Joseph raises his eyebrows. On my first night here, Dad explained how sometimes the Inuit use body language instead of words. Raising your eyebrows like that means "yes." Then the man lifts one mittened hand so it covers his mouth. In Montreal body language, that means there's something he's trying not to say. I don't know what it means here.

Mathilde nudges Dad and then looks over at me.

"Uhh, right," Dad says. "Joseph, this is my son, Noah. I think I mentioned he'd be spending the term with me. Noah, I'm sure you've heard me talk about Joseph. He runs the Individual Path of Learning program over at the school. He works wonders with some of our kids. If it weren't for him, there'd be a lot more kids out of school in this town."

I feel Joseph sizing me up. "You're going to need better mitts than those ones," he says to me, "if you're coming winter camping with me and my students this weekend."

Winter camping? I don't have a problem with summer camping. Summer camping is great. You get to hang out in nature, roast marshmallows and pee in the woods. But camping in minus-thirty-degree weather is another story altogether. Why would anyone want to go out and suffer on the frozen tundra? I mean, what's the point?

Dad and Joseph exchange a look. "Uh," Dad says, "I haven't had a chance to talk to Noah about the winter camping trip yet. He doesn't know you invited the two of us to come along. I've been so darned busy with this dog."

When Dad says the word "dog," Joseph looks over at Tarksalik and shakes his head again. She's still sprawled on the blanket, only now she's started panting, probably from all the exertion. Her belly shakes with every breath. Mathilde is rubbing behind her ears and calling her "beautiful dog" over and over again. If I had to have my knee replaced, I wouldn't want Mathilde for a nurse, not even if she kept telling me what a good-looking guy I was.

Joseph doesn't say a word, but I watch his eyes land on Tarksalik's rump, where the fur is still tufted and encrusted with dried blood. He doesn't ask how the dog is doing. I'm sure he's thinking what everyone else in town besides Dad and Mathilde and me seems to think: that Tarksalik would be better off if we put her out of her misery. That we're making her suffer for nothing.

I think of the vet clinic near my house in Montreal. In the mornings, there's often a lineup of worried-looking people waiting to get in. They've got their cats in carrier cages and some of the dogs wear special dog boots to protect their paws from the snow and salt. Joseph would definitely not approve.

"Listen, Joseph," Dad says, "I'm not going to be able to go camping this weekend. I'm going to have to stay here with Tarksalik. You know, keep an eye on her, make sure she gets her meds." Dad catches Mathilde's eye. "And her exercise."

"Uh-huh," Joseph says. "What about you, Noah? You coming winter camping this weekend?"

A picture of me and Dad—me on the couch, Dad in his armchair with a pile of essays at his feet—flashes through my mind. Tarksalik is lying next to us on her diaper-bed. And Mathilde comes over first thing in the morning to make sure Tarksalik is getting exercise. I can see Tarksalik baring her teeth, then moaning in pain as Mathilde forces her up.

Winter camping is about the last thing on earth I want to do.

No, second to last. The very last thing I want to do is spend a weekend in Dad's dog infirmary.

"Do you think you could manage without me?" I ask Dad.

"Sure thing, Son. No sense in both of us being cooped up here all weekend."

"In that case," I tell Joseph, "count me in."

seven

I spot Steve outside his house when I get home from school the next day. Though it's only four in the afternoon, it's almost completely dark outside. Steve is carrying a plastic bucket. When he sees me, he waves me over.

"Whatcha got there?" I ask, pointing at the bucket. The outside is frosted over.

"Fish heads for the dogs." When Steve exhales, his breath makes a smoky cloud.

I know it'll be gross, but I look inside anyway. The silver fish heads glisten in the dark. Even worse, the fish eyes, glassy and frozen, seem to be staring up at me. My stomach—which has always been what my mom calls "sensitive"—lurches.

"They eat 'em raw?" I manage to ask.

"Absolutely," Steve says. "Fish heads are one of their favorites."

Steve raises Inuit sled dogs. He has a dozen of them living in wooden pens behind his house. Four are pups that were born in the fall. They've still got their soft puppy fur, but their legs are already getting long. I can hear the dogs yapping, probably because they can smell the fish heads.

"Fish heads are high in protein," Steve tells me. "If you catch any Arctic char when you come winter camping with us this weekend, you keep the heads for me, okay?"

"News sure spreads quick in this town," I tell Steve.

"Sure does. But hey, a new guy like you comes to George River, and everyone wants to know his business." Steve's voice turns more serious. "How's Tarksalik?"

"I haven't been back to Dad's yet. Mathilde says Tarksalik needs exercise. Dad's not sure Tarksalik's ready for that."

"Mathilde's probably right," Steve says. "One of my sled dogs got hit last winter. Same sort of accident. Mathilde was a big help."

"What happened to your dog?" My voice cracks. I'm afraid Steve'll say his dog died.

"He's good as new. And I'll tell you one thing: he sure learned to stay away from trucks." Steve pats my shoulder. "Tarksalik's gonna be fine."

I sure hope Steve's right.

Steve isn't the only one in George River who raises sled dogs. Dad told me Joseph is raising them too. It's part of a project to reintroduce Inuit sled dogs to Nunavik. Steve and Joseph think reintroducing Inuit sled dogs might be a way to get the Inuit back in touch with their roots and give them more pride in their culture. "Some of them have trouble with booze. Maybe it'll even help with that," Dad had told me.

"Why do sled dogs have to be *re*introduced anyway?" I ask Steve. The two of us are walking over to the pens behind his house. I'm carrying a bucket now too. The dogs are barking even more now that we're getting closer.

"It's a sad story," Steve says. "You sure you want to hear it?"

"Uh-huh," I tell him. "I wanna know."

Steve sighs. "Well, you need some of the history first. Not too boring for you?"

"Nah, I don't mind."

"When southerners first came to Nunavik, they set up trading posts, like the Hudson's Bay Company. The arrangement wasn't all bad. The Inuit got stuff like rifles, sugar and tea in exchange for fox furs. And though the Inuit still migrated for the hunt, some of them started settling near the trading posts. Matter of fact, that's how George River came to be.

"But the southerners didn't really understand the Inuit's nomadic ways. And I guess it was hard to keep track of people who didn't stay in one place and hard to get them medical care when they needed it. The southerners thought the Inuit would be better off if they had a permanent settlement, so they helped build towns like this one."

Steve and I both stop for a second and look out at the town. There's not much to see. A cluster of prefabricated wooden houses, the school, the clinic, the community center and, in the distance, the gas station. In many of the houses we can see the eerie gray glow from television screens.

Steve takes a breath. The sad part of the story must be coming now. "In the nineteen sixties, the RCMP said the sled dogs were rabid, so they shot them." The words come out flat—Inuit-style—but I can tell from the way the lines on Steve's forehead have tightened that he's upset.

"Shot them?" It's an awful thought.

Steve nods.

"Did they really have rabies?" From the way Steve said it, I already know he's not convinced.

"No one knows for sure, but the Inuit who were around in those days—like Charlie Etok and Matthew Snowflake— insist the dogs weren't sick. They say it was just another way to keep the Inuit in one place. The Inuit relied on those dogs for transportation and to take them out on the hunt. Killing those dogs was like chopping off the Inuit's legs. And you know, some of them still haven't forgiven us."

"*Us?*" I say. "We weren't even up here. I wasn't even born yet."

"Me neither," Steve says, "but like it or not, we're still *Qallunaat*."

"*Qallunaat*," I say, trying out the word. Now I remember that Charlie Etok used that word when he told his legend.

I'm about to ask Steve if he needs help feeding the dogs when Etua comes running out of the house. He's wearing his red and blue Spiderman pajamas again. The kid obviously has a Spiderman fixation.

Steve puts down his bucket of fish heads. "Where's your parka, Etua?" he shouts.

Etua frowns.

"Okay, okay," Steve says. "Where's your parka, Spiderman?"

Etua's face brightens. "Oops," he says, bringing his finger to his mouth, "I forgot it inside. But I just came out for a minute. *Anaana* saw Noah through the window." Etua turns to me. "She says for you to come inside for chocolate-chip cookies. They're hot and they smell really good."

"Get back inside then, Spiderman," Steve says. "And save a couple of those cookies for your old man."

I follow Etua inside. Rhoda is taking a tray of cookies from the oven. Etua is right; they smell really good.

The radio is on in the kitchen, and an announcer is saying something in Inuktitut. "It's going to be super cold this weekend," Rhoda translates for me. "Minus fifty and colder still with the wind. You're going to need to borrow some proper clothes for that winter camping trip."

"You listening to a local station?" I ask Rhoda as she uses a spatula to transfer the hot cookies onto a plate.

"Uh-huh," Rhoda says. "We call it the FM—short for FM radio. It's how we get all our news around here."

The announcer says something else in Inuktitut. There's something I'm starting to like about the sound of the language, even though I have no idea what the words mean. Though Inuktitut sounds flatter than English, it also sounds calmer, as if the people who speak it aren't in a rush, and they don't get too upset about stuff.

Rhoda lets the plate of cookies cool a bit before offering them to Etua and me. We each take one.

"What did the announcer say just now?" I ask her.

Rhoda grins. "He said Lenny Etok's grandma phoned to say if Lenny doesn't get home soon and do his homework, he's not getting any fish for supper tonight."

That cracks me up. "You call that news?" I say.

Rhoda grins. "Around here, it's news."

Etua closes his eyes as he bites into the cookie.

I'm about to take a bite of cookie when I stop myself. For a second, the chocolate chips look just like the fish eyes in Steve's pail.

"Is something wrong?" Rhoda asks me.

"Uh, no," I say. Then I close my eyes the way Etua did and bite into the cookie.

Rhoda wipes her hands on a dishtowel. "You might get to taste seal blubber this weekend," she says.

When Rhoda mentions eating seal blubber, a bit of chocolate-chip cookie catches in my throat. Luckily, I manage to gulp it down. Otherwise, I think I might puke right there on Steve and Rhoda's kitchen floor.

EIGHT

Later that night Dad's doorbell rings, and I open the door to a small Inuit man who shakes my hand Inuit-style. "I heard Bill the teacher had company." He opens his parka and removes a bundle from his inside pocket. He's brought tiny soapstone carvings wrapped in felt. One is shaped like a seal; another like an inukshuk. It takes me a minute to realize this guy is a door-to-door souvenir salesman. In Montreal, the only people who come to sell stuff at our door are kids with chocolate bars for school fundraisers—or Jehovah's Witnesses coming to sell religion on Saturday mornings.

My dad must recognize the carver's voice. "Elijah," Dad calls out from the kitchen, "d'you mind coming back some other time? Noah's going to be with me five whole months. There'll be plenty of time for shopping. Right now's not so good; Tarksalik is having some trouble."

Elijah stuffs the carvings back inside his pocket. He doesn't ask about Tarksalik. When I close the door, he is already heading for the apartment across the hall from Dad's.

"Okay with you if I use your computer?" I ask Dad.

"You don't have to ask," he tells me. "It's your computer too."

FROM: Noah Thorpe [puckU94@quikweb.ca]
TO: Mom
SUBJECT: Hey, Mom

Things here are okay, except Dad's dog got hit by a pickup truck when I took her with me for a run on Tuesday morning. The good news is there don't seem to be any broken bones, and Mathilde, the nurse from the clinic, thinks Tarksalik (that's the dog) will probably be okay. I sure hope she's right!

It's kinda pretty up here in a weird, bleak way. Everywhere you look there's snow—mountains of it—and because we're so close to the tree line, there are hardly any trees—just spindly bushes.

The people are nice enough, only they don't have much to say.

Believe it or not, I'm going winter camping this weekend with one of the teachers from Dad's school and his class of Individual Path of Learning students. (Those are kids who didn't make it in the academic stream, so they study stuff like wilderness skills instead. That way some of them can get jobs as guides after they graduate.)

Dad was supposed to come winter camping, but now he wants to stay home to look after Tarksalik.

Our house in Montreal feels like it's in another world. Dad's okay, and I think he likes it up here. Did he always make so many puns? If so, was that one of the reasons you guys broke up?

I'll write again when I'm back from winter camping—just so you know I survived. (Don't panic! That was a joke.) Love, Noah

P.S. One thing you'd really like about up here is you don't have to leave the house to go shopping. The local carvers come to you. I just saw this little inukshuk you might like. Only Dad and I weren't exactly in a shopping mood.

FROM: Noah Thorpe [puckU94@quikweb.ca]
TO: Chris L'Ecuyer
SUBJECT: Hey dude!

Dude, I can't believe I got sent to this friggin' hellhole. There's nothing to see except snow. And there's nothing to do past 6 pm, except hang out at the grocery store. No wonder some of the kids here spend their free time circling town on their snowmobiles or watching tv or getting wasted.

The worst part is I've got to go winter camping this weekend. It's too complicated to explain why—let's just say staying home with my dad would be even worse than freezing my butt off in a tent and trying to catch my own dinner. What I fear more than running into a polar bear is that the Inuit are gonna force-feed me seal blubber. Apparently, it's a real delicacy up here—kind of like poutine in Montreal, or pretzels in Manhattan.

What's new at home? How's Roland Ikpins doing without me? Has he found someone new to torment? The bad news for me is, even a town as small as this one has got a Roland Ipkins. This one's named Lenny Etok. Same sneer.

Hey, do me a favor and say hi to Tammy Akerman for me, okay? Better still, send me her e-mail address and I'll say hi to her myself.

Write when you can. Noah

Packing List for Winter Camping Trip
long underwear
turtleneck
fleece shirt
snow pants
wool cap
scarf
thermal socks (2 pairs)
snowmobile boots (check with Dad to see if he has an extra pair)
parka (Rhoda said I could borrow Steve's old one)
caribou-hide mitts (ask Steve if I can borrow a pair)
camera (pack camera case inside sock, and sock inside plastic bag, so camera doesn't get wet if it falls in snow)

book
energy bars
flashlight
toothbrush
toothpaste
floss

The packing list turns out to be a good idea. This way,
I don't have to worry about forgetting something important.
Dad has an extra pair of snowmobile boots. Steve lends me
his old parka and a pair of caribou-hide mittens. Too bad
I didn't have the parka and the mitts when I walked into
the Northern the other night; maybe I'd have attracted a
little less attention.

There's only one thing I don't put on the list: beer.
When Dad goes down the street to see if he got any mail,
I grab a few cans from the pile of cases in his front closet.
Dad's not much of a drinker, and I figure chances are good
I'll be back in Montreal before he notices anything's gone
missing.

In Montreal, it's no big deal for a fifteen-year-old to have
a beer. Officially, drinking's not legal in Quebec till you're
eighteen, but most of us have had a few—and sometimes
more than that—at house parties. Last summer, when
Chris's parents were away, his older brother Lee helped us
get a few cases. Man, that was some party! I got a nice buzz
off the beer, and I was brave enough to put my arm around
Tammy Akerman's waist.

It's only now, at the end of the day, when I'm trying to fall asleep, that I start feeling a touch guilty. I'll admit it: stealing your dad's beer is probably not the coolest thing a guy can do. Then again, I was the one who carted it all the way from Montreal. I had to load those cases into Mom's car, check them in at Trudeau Airport, then wait for those babies at Kuujjuaq to make sure they got loaded onto the fifteen-seater Twin Otter plane that brought me (and the beer) to George River.

"Great to see you, Son!" Dad had said, clapping my arm when he met me at the little airport here. "How'd you do on that small plane? Not too bumpy for you?" But Dad didn't wait for me to answer. He was already asking, "Hey, did my beer make it here okay?"

Looking back, I think Dad was more excited when he saw those cases of beer than when he saw me.

The way I see it, Dad owes me the beers I swiped. So I'm not going to feel guilty. Nope, I'm going to lie back and try to get myself some shut-eye. Those beers were part of the deal. They're what I charge for shipping and handling. Family discount included.

nine

Chris and I are walking home after school. Some days, if his mom is on her way back from work, she picks us up. Today she's not waiting at her usual spot. No problem. We're in grade three now. Big enough to walk by ourselves.

Chris and I are carrying the papier-mâché masks we made in art. Chris made a monster with a green face. Mine's a dog. It has pointy ears and a long snout with big black nostrils at the end. The paint on mine isn't completely dry, so I'm waving it in the air while I walk. Wait till Mom sees it. She'll want to hang it up on the wall for sure.

"Hey, you guys, wait for me!" When we turn around, we see Tammy, running to catch up with us, her white-blond hair flapping behind her.

We make room so Tammy can walk between us.

"Nice dog!" she says. Then she looks at Chris's mask. "Scary!"

"Where's yours?" Chris asks.

"It's not dry yet. But I made a princess. With a gold crown and real jewels. Well, real plastic jewels. Miss Brisson attached them with her glue gun. She brought it from home specially for me. That's why my mask's not dry yet."

"Mine's not dry either," I tell Tammy. Tammy makes me nervous because she is so pretty. As pretty as a princess. I like it when she walks home with us.

I hear the thud of heavy footsteps coming up behind us. Even before I look to see who's coming, I feel a pit form at the bottom of my stomach. Don't be Roland Ipkins. Not today. Not now. Not when Tammy Akerman is watching.

I hear Roland's laugh before I see him. It's a mean laugh, just like Roland. He's with his two friends—Eddie Silverstone and Trevor Tait. They're all in grade four. Roland should really be in grade five, but he flunked a grade.

When Roland laughs, Eddie and Trevor laugh too.

Roland sidles up next to me. He's twice my size. "Bringing home your art project to show your mommy?" he calls out. Then he sneers. Roland's sneer makes me nervous too, but not the kind of nervous Tammy Akerman makes me. Roland makes me bad nervous. Pain in my stomach, trembling knees kind of nervous.

When Chris speeds up, so do I. But Tammy stops walking. Uh-oh. Now what do I do? I watch as Tammy puts her hands on her hips and spins around to face Roland and his friends. "Why do you have to be so mean?" she asks Roland.

Chris is walking even faster now. "Come on," he whispers under his breath. He pulls on the sleeve of my sweater, but I shake myself free.

"No," I tell him, "we should wait for Tammy." I stop, but Chris doesn't.

"Why do you hang around with those two losers anyway?" Roland is asking Tammy.

I feel my cheeks get hot when he says that.

"They're not losers. You're the loser," Tammy tells him. My heart is thumping under my white school shirt. Doesn't she know that talking to Roland like that is only going to make him meaner?

"Come on, Tammy," I say. "Let's go."

I flinch when I feel Roland's hand on my shoulder. Roland's teased me before, but this is the first time he's laid a hand on me. We both know I'll go down like a leaf if he hits me. Roland sneers again. The sneer is like a shadow crossing his face. "You wuss," he says, and now I hear the sneer in his voice too. "You need a girl to fight your battles."

"No, I don't," I say, but my voice breaks.

Roland thinks that's funny.

I know I have to hit him. It's what Dad told me to do. "Give him one chop in the stomach and let him know you're tough," he'd said when he was in Montreal at Christmas and we'd gone out for burgers. I hadn't meant to tell Dad about Roland, but the story just spilled out.

I make a fist. Because Roland is so much taller than me, I'll have to reach up to hit him in the belly. Then Roland says something else.

"How come you don't have a dad?"

The question takes me by surprise. I drop my hand back to my side. "I do too have a dad."

"Maybe that's why he needs a girl to fight his battles," Eddie says.

Trevor laughs. But it's Roland who grabs the dog mask out of my hand. I make another fist, a tighter one. I'm aiming for Roland's belly when a weird thing happens.

It's not Roland anymore. I know, because he's not wearing his Habs cap. He's wearing a red *nassak*. And the hair sticking out from under it isn't dark and curly, like Roland's. This hair is dark, but very, very straight.

I'm looking into Lenny Etok's eyes. What's he doing in Montreal? Lenny grabs the mask from my hand and tosses it on the ground, laughing. Then he stomps on it. The papier-mâché breaks into a hundred pieces.

When I try to hit him, Lenny moves away, and I miss his belly altogether.

"Stop it! Don't fight!" a girl's voice cries out. Now I'm even more confused. It's Geraldine Snowflake, not Tammy Akerman. And there are dogs too. Lots of them. Inuit sled dogs. Jumping into the air, barking and biting at my ankles. Tarksalik is there too. Only she's not jumping or barking or biting at my ankles. She's crying—human tears. This isn't making any sense; dogs don't cry. Or do they?

"Leave me alone!" I shout, but the dogs pay no attention.

"Stop it! Stop it right now!" Geraldine says. I can't tell who she's talking to. Me and Lenny, or the dogs? That's when

I notice there is a breast growing out of Geraldine's cheek. The nipple is brown and hairy. Though it's the grossest thing I've ever seen, I can't stop looking at it.

Tarksalik begins to howl.

"I'm sorry!" I tell her.

Tarksalik can't hear me over the sound of her own howling, so I say it even louder. "I'm sorry!"

The sound of my own voice wakes me up. It's so cold in here. Where am I, anyhow? In Montreal? No, that doesn't make any sense. Oh, yeah. I'm at Dad's house in George River. I must've kicked off the covers in my sleep, and now I pull them up over me. There, that's better.

The red numbers on the clock radio next to me read 3:15. That was one weird dream, I think, as I try to fall back to sleep. Dogs don't cry like that. And girls don't have breasts growing out of their cheeks.

ten

By the time the alarm on the clock radio goes off at seven in the morning, I can hardly remember the dream. Only that it was weird, and that Roland Ipkins morphed into Lenny Etok. Wasn't there something about a dog too? When I try to reach back into my mind to remember more, the whole thing disappears. No big deal, I tell myself, it was just a dream. A dumb weird dream.

I say good-bye to Tarksalik before I leave Dad's apartment to go winter camping. Though Mathilde keeps saying Tarksalik is getting better, she still looks pretty bad to me. The fur near her hind legs is just as matted as it was after the accident, and when I pet her head, she makes a whinnying sound as if she's in a dream too—one she doesn't want to wake up from.

It's still dark out. I decide not to wake Dad. It's the first night all week he's slept in his bed instead of in his armchair next to Tarksalik. I leave him a note saying I'll see him and Tarksalik Sunday night.

When I look out the front window, I notice the lights are on at Steve and Rhoda's. It's 5:40. Steve told me to be at their place a little before six. But because I can't think of anything better to do, I grab my backpack and head over.

Steve is busy loading his sled with supplies in waterproof packs and coolers. It's kind of ironic using coolers up here; when you think about it, Nunavik is one giant cooler.

"You can help me get the dogs ready," Steve calls when he sees me crossing the road.

The dogs must sense they're about to head off on an adventure. Each dog has its own pen, which is basically a simple wooden doghouse. Every pen is enclosed inside its own large wire cage. The cages are about twice the size of the pens. The dogs have left their pens and are pressing their front legs up against the wire. One starts howling, and soon the rest join in. A couple leap into the air as if they can't wait to leave.

Steve laughs. "Okay, kids," he says, "we're almost ready."

"Hey, Toto," Steve says, when he unlatches the cage closest to us. Toto is huge, nothing like the little mutt in *The Wizard of Oz*. Toto rushes out of his cage, practically mowing Steve down. The dog leans forward so Steve can attach him to the fan hitch, a bunch of giant leather leads designed to hold an entire team of dogs. It's called a fan because the leads fan out from the hitch. The fan hitch keeps the dogs spread out and prevents them from bumping into each other or fighting.

"Here, hang onto these leads for me," Steve says. "Toto here is the one I told you about. He doesn't like pickup trucks."

It's hard to imagine Tarksalik ever being well enough to pull a dogsled, but then I remember how Steve said Toto was in pretty bad shape, too, after he got hit by a truck.

Steve lets another sled dog out of its cage. This one's a girl, but she's strong-looking.

Steve shows me how to attach her to the harness. "The Inuit invented the fan harness. If a dog gets tangled in his lead, there's enough room for him to get untangled. And if one dog falls through the ice, the others don't end up in the river too."

His words make me shiver. It's hard to imagine anyone lasting very long in a river up here, even if they're really good swimmers and have fur coats the way dogs do.

Steve takes my elbow and hurries me past the next pen. "We'll get P'tit Eric last."

P'tit Eric is the leader of the pack. He's even bigger than the others, and when he jumps against the bars of his cage, the ground vibrates. Steve explains that once P'tit Eric is attached to the harness, there'll be no stopping him or the other dogs. "He's a natural born puller," Steve says. "The others follow his lead."

I almost don't recognize Etua when he comes running out of the house. "How come you're not wearing your Spiderman pajamas?" I ask him.

"They're in here," he says, throwing his backpack onto the toboggan. Spiderman's on the backpack too.

"Ever gone out with a dog team before?" Steve asks me as he fastens another dog to one of the leads. He rubs the dog's muzzle.

"Nope, never. Dad said it could be a bumpy ride."

"Bumpy, yes," Steve says. "But that's part of the fun."

When it's time to let P'tit Eric out of his cage, Steve crouches low to the ground to get a good grip on the scruff of the dog's neck. P'tit Eric's ears prick up, and he sniffs the air. As soon as the other dogs spot him, they let out a chorus of wild howls. *A-ooh, a-ooh! A-ooh, a-ooh!* So much for anybody's plans to sleep in on a Saturday morning!

The sled dogs will probably wake up Tarksalik too. I wonder if she feels bad that Steve's dog team is about to head off into the tundra and she's going to spend the weekend lying on the floor in Dad's apartment. Tarksalik's not a sled dog, but Dad told me she likes to come when he and Steve go winter camping. She's fast enough to keep up with Dad's snowmobile. At least she *used* to be fast enough.

"I'm going to mush," Steve explains. "You and Etua are gonna sit behind me on the *qamutik*. You keep an eye on Etua, okay? Don't let him fall off." He pokes Etua in the stomach. "Your *anaana*'ll never forgive me if I lose you."

Steve turns back to me. "I want you to watch what I'm doing too. You might get to do some mushing before this weekend's over."

"Sounds great," I say, trying to sound excited. What I'm really thinking is, I hope I'm not going to end up in the river like some human Popsicle.

Steve arranges the dogs so they're fanned out against the snow. There's some barking, but mostly they stay where he positions them. Etua makes a spot for me next to him at the back of the *qamutik*. I try not to think how, four days ago, Tarksalik was lying right where I am now sitting.

There's no sign of the blue and black plaid blanket with the blue fringes. I wonder whether Steve and Rhoda were able to wash out the bloodstains.

Steve steps onto the front of the *qamutik* and yells out something that sounds like "*Oyt!*"

That sound must mean "Go!" because as soon as he says it, the dogs are off! For a couple of seconds, the *qamutik* scrapes against the hard-packed snow, and then—*whoosh!*—we're flying past houses and bushes and the path that leads to the school. Man, can these dogs ever pull! We must be going almost as fast as a car, and we're not burning gasoline and destroying the Earth's ozone layer while we're at it.

Etua cries out, "*Oyt! Oyt!*" too. I just laugh, a deep long laugh that comes from the bottom of my belly and makes me feel more relaxed than I've felt since I came to George River. The cold air isn't hurting my lungs; right now, it just feels good. Energizing. When we reach a bump in the road, our *qamutik* flies way up in the air.

Up we go! A foot at least, maybe more. No wonder Steve used bungee cord to tie down the packs and coolers! All this *qamutik* is missing is seatbelts!

"*Oyt! Oyt!*" Etua and I shout together. It feels good to shout so loud.

The dogs pull even harder. *Whap!* The *qamutik* lands back on the snow, making a crashing sound as it hits the ground. I can feel my butt slap down against the wooden base of the *qamutik*. Something tells me my butt is going to be black and blue by Sunday night.

It would take twenty minutes at least to walk to the edge of town, but the dogs get us there in under five. The wind whips against our cheeks, and Etua's dark eyes are shining. Right now, I'm having too much fun to notice how cold it is.

The houses, which are crowded next to each other in the center of town where Dad and Steve and his family live, become more spread out, and soon there aren't any houses at all. Just snow. Mountains of it. This is what the moon must look like in winter.

When the road comes to an end, we switch to a narrow path. I can see the tracks snowmobiles have left in the snow. Who needs a snowmobile, I think, when you can travel by dogsled?

I can't help feeling disappointed when Steve tugs hard on the harness and the dogs slow to a stop. The wind is picking up; the sky is still completely dark. We've reached the first bend. I hear barking in the distance. P'tit Eric's dark ears prick up again. Some of the other dogs are panting, their purple tongues hanging out of their mouths. Maybe they need a rest, but not P'tit Eric.

Two more dogsled teams—one is Joseph's—are meeting us here.

Joseph's team turns up first. His dogs growl when they get close to Steve's team. P'tit Eric bares his teeth, then Steve's other dogs start growling too. I hope this isn't going to turn into a dogfight. But Joseph takes charge. "Hey," he says sternly, and all the dogs, even Steve's, settle down, though they are still eyeing each other as if they are not quite sure whether the other team can be trusted.

Joseph nods when he sees me. "Ay, Noah," he says, "these are a couple of my IPL students." He turns to the two boys riding on his *qamutik*. "Tom and Roy." Both boys nod at me. I notice Tom's eyes aren't as dark as the others. Maybe he has *Qallunaaq* blood in him.

Now another dogsled team pulls up next to Joseph's. These dogs are a little smaller than the others and less aggressive. A couple of them try to sniff one of the dogs at the back of Joseph's team. When the dog growls, the smaller ones back off, their tails between their legs. Their musher is a tall Inuit boy with flushed cheeks. "This here is Jakopie," Joseph says. "He's IPL too. Jakopie has his own small dogsled team. This is their first long trip. That's why Jakopie only has one passenger." Jakopie's passenger has his back to me. "I think you know Lenny from school."

Just my luck. I'm going to be spending the weekend with Lenny Etok.

Lenny turns and smirks at me from the back of Jakopie's *qamutik*.

"Lenny's not an IPL student," I say.

"Neither are you," Lenny says.

He has a point there.

Etua gets off our *qamutik*. "Dad," he says, jumping up and down as he speaks, "Can I ride with cousin Roy?"

"It's okay by me—as long as the other guys don't mind switching places."

Etua and I are the only ones without rifles slung across our chests. Because they're Inuit, or like Steve, married to an Inuk, they have hunting permits.

Tom slides off Joseph's *qamutik* to give Etua his spot. Then Tom comes over to our *qamutik*. "Nice to meet you." He reaches for my hand. By now, I don't expect a proper shake. "So you come from the south," Tom says as he sits down next to me.

"I guess I do. I'm just not used to thinking of Montreal as south of anyplace. In Montreal, south usually means Florida or maybe Mexico."

Tom grins. "Just about the whole world is south of George River," he says.

Joseph's glasses are fogged over from the cold. He wipes at them with his mitts, then reaches into his pocket for what turns out to be a battery-operated GPS. "Let's review our route," he says to Steve.

Soon we're off again. Our team is up front; Jakopie's is in the middle, followed by Joseph's. When I turn to look behind me, all I can make out is a blur of dogs—ears and muzzles and legs and torsos and tails—all flying over the snow.

I tug on my ski tuque so it'll cover more of my forehead. I'm the only one who isn't wearing a *nassak*. Still, my tuque has got to be warmer than their *nassaks*, which don't even cover the bottoms of their ears. Maybe people up here are just more used to the cold.

I wiggle my toes inside the boots Dad lent me. They're a touch big, but I wore an extra pair of socks to make up for it. Despite the cold, my toes are still moving. I figure that's a good sign.

There's a thin, pale-blue band of sky over the river now. There's snow everywhere else, with a few scraggly bushes here and there. Not the best place to live on planet Earth if you happen to be a bush.

From my spot on the *qamutik*, all I can see now of Steve's dogs are their rumps and hind legs. As they run, they leave a trail of watery, blackish brown droppings on the snow behind them.

"What's tha—?" I start to ask Tom, but I stop in midsentence. Those droppings are shit. Dog shit. All that pulling must make the dogs crap. Talk about gross! I think back to the Kuujjuaq Airport, where they were selling postcards with pictures of dog teams. Only in those postcards dogs weren't crapping all over the snow!

Tom must've figured out what I was about to ask, because he cracks up. "It's part of life, man," he says, his eyes crinkling at the corners when he smiles.

Part of life. Wasn't that what Geraldine said about the avalanche?

"Hey, you guys," Steve shouts from the front of the *qamutik*, without turning around to look at us. "We're coming to a bit of a hill."

"That means we're gonna have to jump off and run with the dogs," Tom explains.

"Jump off? Run with the dogs?" I look up ahead; to me, that "bit of a hill" looks more like a small mountain. A very steep small mountain.

But there's no one to answer my questions. Tom has jumped off the *qamutik* and he's already running to catch up with the dogs. I can hear him up ahead, panting.

So I jump too. Only by then, we've started climbing the hill and somehow, instead of landing in a pile of snow, I crash face-first into a snowbank. And because I didn't expect that to happen, I end up losing my footing and falling backward, landing in a bed of powder snow. Man, is it cold!

Dad's boots weigh me down, and when I try to pull myself up, one of the boots comes loose. Even two layers of thermal socks aren't helping to protect me from the cold now. "Crap!" I call out, dancing on one foot as I reach into the snow for the missing boot. Now the snow is getting inside my mitts too. Man, this sucks! And where the hell did that boot get to? It's got to be here somewhere.

Jakopie's dog team pushes past me. A couple of dogs turn their heads when they spot me in the snowbank. It's a bad feeling when you think dogs are laughing at you.

I feel even worse a couple of seconds later, when Lenny sees me in the snowdrift. By then, I've found the missing boot and am trying to get it back on without losing my balance and getting my foot even wetter.

With the dogs, I only had the feeling they were laughing at me. With Lenny, I'm sure he is.

He's running alongside Jakopie's dogs as if it's the most natural thing in the world. "Can't keep up with Inuit dogs?" he calls out as he passes me.

eleven

"We're stopping for lunch," Steve shouts. "It's time for a rest."

A rest sounds good to me. Jogging in the city is nothing compared to running in heavy too-big boots alongside a dogsled team, and the powder snow only makes it tougher. Not to mention two of the four thermal socks I'm wearing are still soaking wet. Wet and cold is a bad combination. A very bad combination.

Luckily, we're on a flat stretch, so Tom and I are sitting again. I hope he can't tell I'm still trying to catch my breath.

I can feel Tom watching me. "Can I ask you something?" he finally asks.

"Sure, ask away."

Tom hesitates for a moment. "Did you ever have a Big Mac?"

I try not to laugh. "Sure," I tell him. "All the time."

Tom nods slowly. I can tell there's another question coming, even if it may take a while. The Inuit don't seem to do anything in a rush. "So what do Big Macs taste like, anyhow?"

"Like a hamburger, but with a special sauce on it," I tell him. "The bun's a little soggy though. I guess you've never had one, right?"

Tom raises his eyebrows to say yes. Or in this case, no. He's never had a Big Mac. "Me and my family eat mostly country food—stuff we trap or catch. And sometimes junk food from the Northern or the Co-op. Except for camping trips like this one, I've never left George River." From the way he says it, it's hard to tell whether he thinks never leaving George River is a good thing or a bad thing.

For a second, I try to imagine what that would feel like, but I can't. I've lived in Montreal all my life, but it's a big city with millions of people, and I've traveled to other places, like New York and Toronto and even Cuba. The idea of never leaving George River makes me feel kind of claustrophobic. It's a weird feeling, considering how everywhere I look there's nothing but snow and empty space. And loads of it. If I had to spend my entire life up here, away from everything Montreal has to offer—the Bell Centre, movie theaters, restaurants, stores, tons of people—I'd feel trapped. But if Tom's never been anywhere else, he can't know what he's missing.

"I'll buy you a Big Mac when you come to Montreal," I tell him.

Tom grins. "Did you ever eat ptarmigan?" he asks.

"Until Tuesday night, I never even heard of ptarmigan."

"I guess ptarmigan's kind of like our Big Mac. Only we don't have to line up for ptarmigan. Or pay. We just shoot 'em."

"You shoot 'em?"

"Yup," Tom says, adjusting the rifle that is slung over his shoulder, "then we roast 'em for lunch. You'll probably be eating some today. The heart and liver are the best parts. We eat those raw."

I gulp. "Raw?"

Tom licks his lips.

Maybe I should have stayed with Dad and Tarksalik after all.

"How far are we from Short Lake now?" I ask Tom when we begin slowing down.

Tom turns to look out at the tundra. "Coupla hours at most," he says. "You'll know we're almost there when we see the inukshuk."

I pat the camera in my pocket. My mom will want a picture of the inukshuk. She has a collection of miniature inukshuks on a shelf at home, and I helped her build one in our front yard.

The dog teams pull up near a small wooden cabin just beyond the trail. The cabin has a porch that wraps around two sides. "One of the teachers built it himself," Tom explains as we climb off the qamutik. "He moved back south. But he left Steve the key."

"Why would anyone go to the trouble of building a cabin up here?"

Tom shrugs. "I guess he wanted some place quiet to come to."

I look to see whether Tom is joking, but he isn't. "Some place quieter than George River? Isn't George River already in the middle of friggin' nowhere?"

I'm sorry I said it almost as soon as the words are out of my mouth. Tom puts his hand to his chest, like I've slugged him. "It's not the middle of nowhere to us," he says, looking right at me. "For us, George River is the middle of everywhere."

We have to wade through the snow to reach the cabin. By the time we get there, Jakopie has already lit the wood-stove. Steve is trying to help Etua unzip his parka, but Etua wants to do it himself. I'm beginning to realize that Etua is a very stubborn kid.

"Your dogs are looking real good," Steve tells Jakopie.

For a second, I notice Jakopie's dark eyes light up, but then he looks back down at the snow. You can tell he isn't used to compliments. "I do my best with 'em" is all he says. He pokes at the fire, but I think he's just trying to keep busy. Jakopie's even quieter than the other Inuit.

"Joseph says you've been doing a lot of fishing and hunting so your dogs have food."

"Uh-huh," Jakopie says. "A lot of fishing and hunting. Carving too. Joseph's been teaching me how. He says he might be able to help me sell some of my carvings to this gallery in Quebec City. That'd help pay for dog food when I have trouble getting country food. If I can keep away from cigarettes like I been trying to, I'll save even more money."

Jakopie takes a deep breath, as if he needs to come up for air after all that talking.

"Sounds like a good plan," Steve tells him. "You must be a pretty good carver if Joseph offered to help you out like that. Those dogs are lucky to have you, Jakopie. Darn lucky."

This time, Jakopie doesn't say anything. But when he smiles, I notice that one of his front teeth is broken right in half. I run my tongue across my own front teeth. I never realized before that I was lucky to have them.

I hear a popping sound outside, followed by another and then two more, one right after the other. "I guess Lenny and Tom are shooting our lunch," Steve tells me. "Looks like we need some more wood for the stove. Can I put you in charge of that, Noah?"

"Sure," I say, though what I'm really thinking is my body hasn't defrosted yet. What I'd really like to do is peel off my wet socks and let them dry on the stove.

"You might have to scrounge around for wood. There'll be some good-sized spruce trees up by the lake, but there's just small shrubs around here," Steve says.

Now why didn't I think of that?

The skin on my fingers is dry and chapped. I bring my hands to my mouth and blow on them. Then I put my mitts back on, toss on my parka and head out. Before I go, I take one last look at the woodstove.

Outside, the wind whistles past me. I look down at the dogs. They're by the trail, spread out on the hard-packed snow. Only P'tit Eric is still on his feet, sniffing the air.

We might have needed a rest, but P'tit Eric looks like he'd have preferred to keep running.

I spot some of the small shrubs Steve was talking about. They're not far from the cabin, but I have to wade through more snow to reach them. I grab whatever twigs I can find. Soon one pocket of my parka is full. This is going to be easier than I thought.

I hear more popping sounds. Some of the dogs start barking. Maybe they're hoping to have ptarmigan for lunch too.

"Hey, Noah!" a voice shouts. It's Tom. "Come see what we got!"

I'm glad Mom isn't around. She loves birds. She keeps a pair of binoculars on the back porch in case any interesting ones come around. She goes nuts if she sees a cardinal or a blue jay, even a yellow finch. Once she woke me up to show me a woodpecker in our backyard. I bet Mom's never even heard of ptarmigan.

Tom and Lenny are standing in a clearing on the other side of the cabin. On the ground in front of them is a long row of dead birds. The boys have laid them out neatly against the snow. The birds have furry-looking feet. Their feathers are white and gray—the colors of the tundra. There's red too, but that's from their blood, which is spattered near them on the snow.

I count the birds. "Ten," I say. "That was quick."

Lenny makes a grunting sound. "It's easy. They're stupid birds," he says. "They don't even try to fly away when they see us coming."

"Look at this one!" Tom grins as he lifts one of the birds from the snow, picking him up by the neck. "I shot him right through the head. Means I didn't waste any meat."

Tom plucks three feathers from the bird's tail. "For good luck," he says, handing Lenny and me each a pale white feather, and keeping one for himself.

I'm not quite sure what I'm supposed to do with the feather. So when Lenny puts his into the front pocket of his parka, I do the same. "Thanks," I tell Tom.

Lenny points over at the shrubs. The sun's come out and I have to shade my eyes to see. There's a ptarmigan, sunning himself. Lenny hands me his rifle. "Wanna shoot him?"

"But I don't have a license."

"We're not going to tell anyone. C'mon. Don't you wanna try?"

I can't say no. Not if I don't want Lenny thinking I'm a wuss. I take the rifle. It's lighter than I expected. Then I take a step forward and aim right at the bird. I pull back on the trigger. Just as I shoot, the bird flies off. Soon all I see is a spot of gray and white against the blue sky. I'm part relieved, part disappointed.

I hand the rifle back to Lenny. "I thought you said it was easy."

"It's easy for us. You got too close," he mutters.

Tom reaches into the pocket of his snow pants for his knife. Then he kneels down and slices open the bird he's holding. He pulls on the membrane that separates the skin from the meat. The breast meat is deep red, much redder than chicken.

I know I can't look away. I remember how we dissected a pig in biology last year and I nearly puked. I haven't eaten a pork chop since.

Tom reaches into the bird's guts to pull out the heart and liver. The heart is small and bright red; the liver, almost black. The heat they give off makes the air misty. Just a few minutes ago, that heart was pumping inside the ptarmigan, and the liver was doing whatever it is livers do.

Tom slices the heart and liver into three pieces each. He pops his share into his mouth, then passes Lenny his share.

My turn's next. Tom passes me the two small slivers of meat. Bright red ptarmigan blood drips from his lips.

I want to close my eyes, but I know I can't. So I take the two pieces of meat and pop them into my mouth. I try thinking of a Big Mac—the tangy sauce, the soggy bun.

Lenny rolls his eyes. "You've got to chew on it, man," he says.

So I do. I chew hard. The heart goes down okay. At first, I don't think I'll mind the liver either. I try to enjoy the warm sensation in my mouth. But then I taste blood—sharp and metallic.

Thinking about a Big Mac isn't working now. Instead, all I can think about is that I'm eating raw bird's liver. And even though I'm not looking at Tom anymore, I can still picture the blood dripping from his lips.

That's when I puke.

Tom claps my back and offers to get me some water. "There's some on Steve's *qamutik*," he says.

Lenny laughs so hard he falls over in the snow.

TWELVE

The others eat ptarmigan for lunch. I wait for my stomach to settle. Then I have half a cheese sandwich and a few bites of a granola bar with chocolate chips. *Small bites. Chew well!* I can almost hear Mom's voice.

The cabin, which was ice cold when we came in, has warmed up quickly, thanks to the fire and our body heat. At first, I leave my parka and mitts on, but soon I take them off. My wet socks are already hanging on a makeshift clothesline over the stove. The smoke from the fire stings my eyes.

Lenny is roasting chunks of breast meat over the fire. "You sure you don't want to try some more?" he asks me.

"I'm sure."

"You still look a little green, Noah," Steve says, shaking his head.

The cabin we've come to belongs to a guy named Jean. It turns out he was senior English teacher at the school before Dad came to George River. The cabin's pretty simple.

There's only one room. It smells musty, and you can't really call what's in it furniture. The couch is the backseat of someone's truck, only it has two orange-and-yellow crocheted pillows on it, which you don't usually find in a truck. The table's a plywood box and the bookshelves are made from pink plastic milk crates. There are a lot of books in those crates: a dusty encyclopedia, a collection of fairy tales from around the world and a pile of how-to books. *How to Build a Garage: 12 Easy Steps. How to Do Your Own Plumbing.* Since the cabin doesn't have either a garage or plumbing, I figure Jean never got around to reading those two.

There are photographs, too, on the crates and on the plywood box. A bare-chested man in shorts with a small kid on either side. Pictures of him with the same kids looking more grown-up. The man, grinning, with his arms around the kids' shoulders.

"Where's Jean now?" I ask Steve.

"Went back to Toronto. Too bad. He was a lot of fun. When we used to stop here on our way to camp, he'd be waiting for us. The fire would be roaring, and he'd have a pot of tomato soup going. He always said it was homemade, his secret recipe. The funny thing is, after he left we found a whole pile of soup cans out back. Campbell's Tomato." The memory makes Steve chuckle.

"If he liked it so much up here, why'd he leave?" I ask.

"Maybe he ran out of Campbell's Tomato," Tom jokes.

"Nah, that's not why," Steve says. "Jean missed his kids too much to stay up north for good. Said he didn't feel right being so far away from them."

I bite my lip. The vomit has left a sour taste in my mouth. Water helped, but not enough.

Steve must know what I'm thinking. "I'm sure it's hard for your dad too."

I unwrap the second half of the cheese sandwich from the waxed paper it's packed in. "I guess we never lived together long enough for him to miss me," I say.

"That must've been tough for both of you," Steve says.

Lenny's sitting on the floor at the other end of the room, eating roast ptarmigan. But he's listening. I know, because he mutters, "At least you've got a dad."

Does that mean Lenny doesn't? But when I turn to look at him, he's concentrating on his ptarmigan, gnawing the last slivers of meat off the bone. The Inuit sure don't let a thing go to waste.

Etua pulls at the sleeve of the fleece jacket I wore under my parka. "Can you play yet? I'll be Spiderman. You try to catch me, okay?"

"Give Noah some time to let his belly settle," Steve tells Etua.

Etua is quiet for about three seconds. "Is your belly settled yet?" he asks me.

"Not quite," I tell him.

"Lenny told me I should make you play with me. He said it'd be good for your belly."

Steve sighs. "Lenny thought he was being funny." Steve says this loudly so Lenny will hear him. Tom is squatting next to Lenny. Jakopie is sitting on the floor too, in the same position. I don't understand how the Inuit can stay sitting like that for so long. My legs would kill. Jakopie is whittling a piece of caribou antler. I wonder what he's making, but I'm still too queasy to ask.

Joseph hands me a mug of steaming tea. "It's Labrador tea," he says, winking. "Good for your belly."

I bring the tea to the couch. There are burn holes in the vinyl, but I figure it'll be better than sitting on the cold floor. Sitting down on the couch is more work than I expected. My thighs ache from running with the dogs. When I finally sit, my body starts to relax. Squatting on the floor to eat might be an Inuit custom, but couches and chairs are more my style. Besides, somebody went to the trouble of inventing those things, so why not take advantage, right?

"I think your old man's pretty cool," Lenny says, without turning to look at me.

Cool isn't the first word I'd use to describe my dad. Goofy, maybe. A little boring. But not cool. Definitely not. But I don't want to tell Lenny that. "He's okay," I say.

"He tells good stories," Lenny says.

Yeah, I think, if you don't mind the puns or how he tries to turn everything into an educational opportunity.

"Yeah," Tom joins in. "Like that story about how he spent the night on a rock ledge when he was a kid. That was pretty cool." Tom slaps his thigh.

I take a sip of tea. It tastes like leaves and dirt. Still, compared to ptarmigan liver, it's delicious. "Rock ledge?" I say. "My dad slept on a rock ledge?" I can't picture Dad anywhere near a rock ledge. Where would he go to do his morning stretches?

"Yeah," Lenny says, and now his voice starts to sound a little more excited. "He was with a friend from school and they were out on a day hike. In New York State, I think he said. Only there was a bad storm, and him and the friend got stranded. They ended up sleeping on a rock ledge. Your dad said it wasn't more than about two feet wide." Lenny uses his hands to demonstrate. "He said if he rolled over, he would've fallen off and died. Your dad said he was scared out of his mind, but he also said that, when he thinks back on it, it was one of the best nights of his life—sleeping under the stars and all."

I can sense one of my dad's lessons coming. Something about how sometimes time has to go by before you can appreciate the stuff that happens to you. Or maybe something about how it's easier to get through tough times when there's a friend with you. But Lenny doesn't say anything about lessons. "When your dad told us that story, he made us feel like we were right there with him. Shivering on the ledge, afraid to turn around, you know?"

This time, when I take another sip of tea, it gets caught in my throat. I gulp to make it go down. "Funny," I say, "my dad never told me that story."

THIrTeen

The inukshuk towers over the tundra, and with so little else to see except snow and rocks and bushes, we spotted it when we were still some distance from Short Lake. Now, with the sun's last rays reflecting off it, the inukshuk will make a great picture.

I have to take off my caribou-skin mitts to get the camera out of my parka's inside pocket. I'm glad I thought of packing the camera case inside a sock inside a plastic bag, otherwise, the lens would be frosted over by now. We left Jean's cabin just after 11:00 AM for the second leg of our trip, and now it's after 2:00 PM. The dogs are slowing down. Even P'tit Eric is panting.

The sky is beginning to grow dark. There are navy and gray swirls of cloud building their way up from the horizon. In an hour or so, there won't be any light left at all. This time of year, Nunavik doesn't get more than five or six hours of daylight. At least I wasn't up here in December.

I'd have lost my mind. "No wonder bears hibernate," I say out loud.

"Not polar bears," Tom mutters. He must have heard me talking to myself. He's off the *qamutik* too, stretching his legs.

My fingers are so cold they burn. But I want to take a picture of the inukshuk for my mom. I tell the others about the little inukshuk in our yard in Montreal, how we made it from stones Mom bought at the gardening center.

"What's a gardening center?" Etua asks.

Mom's inukshuk is about a foot and a half high. This one is about twenty times bigger.

"Nice camera," Tom says. "It's one of those SLRs, right?"

"Uh-huh." I don't know if Tom has ever seen an SLR camera before.

I hand it to him. "It's auto-everything."

Tom whistles as he peers into the lens.

"See the screen? That's what your picture's gonna look like. Go ahead—try it out."

"You sure?"

"I'm sure."

Tom points the camera at the inukshuk and shoots.

"You need to press down harder."

"I don't want to break it."

"You're not gonna break it."

"You sure?"

"I'm sure."

Tom whistles when I set the camera to *Display* and he sees his picture.

"See," I tell him, "you shoot better with a camera than I do with a rifle."

When Tom laughs, I feel good, but then it occurs to me I just made a pun. I hope it doesn't mean I'm turning into my dad.

Etua has come to join us. "Here, Noah," he says, "I have something for you." He hands me two worn gray stones. They look like quartz.

"Where'd you find them?" I ask him.

"Near the cabin. I'm going to save them for your mom, for her inukshuk," he says.

"Great idea. Great Spiderman idea."

Etua's chest puffs up. "I'll try to find more," he says.

Just then, Joseph and his dog team pull up next to where we're standing. I feel him watching me, noticing my camera. "Inukshuk is Inuktitut for 'standing man,'" he says.

The inukshuk really does look like a standing man with huge stumpy legs like Kajutaijug's.

"We build inukshuks as markers. That one has been here for as long as I can remember. Inukshuks are meant to say to hunters, 'You're on the right path.'" Joseph gazes out at the inukshuk.

"The right path, huh?" I say as I shoot another picture.

I'm not so sure I'm on the right path. Mom sent me to Nunavik to get closer to my dad, but here I am, on a winter camping trip with a group of people I didn't even know a week ago. Right now, I feel as far away from my dad as I did when I was in Montreal and he was up here.

"That's it," Joseph says, pointing in the distance. "Short Lake. I can hear the fish—well, almost." He chuckles.

Though the lake is blanketed with snow, you can tell it's a lake because it's as flat as a tabletop and there are no rocks or bushes jutting up from its surface. I can just make out a small forest of spruce trees in a valley near the lake's edge.

When we're back on the dogsleds and have traveled a little farther, I see what looks like a miniature town. Only instead of houses, there are canvas tents, clusters of four or five of them set up in small inlets around the lake. The spruce trees seem to grow in clusters too. The people who set up the tents must have tried to take advantage of whatever shelter the trees provide from the wind and snow.

I count nine tents. Every tent has a chimney, so the tents must be set up for the season. Puffs of blackish gray smoke are already billowing out of one tent. There's a snowmobile parked outside too. No wonder they made better time than us!

"I don't get it," I say to Tom as we help Steve unload supplies. "If the idea of winter camping is to get away from town, how come you guys come all this way just to make a new town?"

Tom looks surprised by my question. "Out here, people need to stick together," he says.

"Come on, guys!" Steve calls. "Let's move on the unpacking! I'm going to need your help setting the lines. I promised the dogs fresh Arctic char for breakfast!"

I grab a cooler from the back of the sled and follow Tom to one of the tents. We crouch to get through the opening, but once we're inside, the tent is roomier than I expect. It doesn't have a window, but I can see out by looking through the narrow crack where the door zips up. In the distance, I spot someone out on the lake, fishing, probably.

The air inside the tent smells like spruce. That's probably because the floor is covered with spruce needles and bits of twigs that crunch under our feet when we bring in the supplies. There are foam mattresses piled up at one end; at the other end, I spot a black metal stove hooked up to a tin chimney. "We built that stove," Tom tells me when he sees me eyeing it. "It was an IPL project." I also see dice, a deck of cards with frayed edges and a felt bag that looks like it might have dominoes inside.

"Hey, Noah," a girl's voice calls from the opening of the tent.

What's Geraldine doing up here? Against the snowy landscape, her hair looks even darker.

"Hey, Geraldine, don't you work at the Northern on the weekends?"

"I got this weekend off to go fishing with my dad. Our tent's just down there," she says, pointing to the one that has smoke billowing out of its chimney.

"Awesome," I tell her.

I notice that Geraldine's smile is a little lopsided. "Uh-huh," she says. "Awesome."

fourteen

It's only when I'm wrapped inside my sleeping bag that the images from Tarksalik's accident come back: her body flying up in the air, the red pickup truck taking off, her blood on the snow-covered road.

I'm amazed that I didn't think about the accident all day. I was too busy fighting the cold, helping with the dogs and the fishing net. We worked into the dark, and now I hardly have the energy to turn over. Winter camping's even harder work than I expected.

Just fall asleep, I tell myself. I can hear Tom snoring lightly on the mattress next to mine. He even sleeps in squatting position—his legs folded under him, his chest and head stretched out in front of him so that his forehead touches the mattress. Lenny sleeps on his side, southern-style. The two of them conked right out. If only that would happen to me too.

I wish I could talk to my dad. Steve has a satellite phone—a clunky thing that must weigh three pounds—but it's only for emergencies, so I haven't had the heart to ask whether I could use it to call Dad and see how Tarksalik is doing. Besides, I can imagine the look Lenny would give me if he hears I'm still worried about the dog.

If I talked to my dad, maybe I'd also say something about that night he slept on the rock ledge. Maybe I'd ask why he never told me that story and why he told the kids in George River more about himself than he ever told me. But who am I kidding? I'd never say any of that to my dad. I'd ask about Tarksalik and then maybe we'd talk about the weather or how many assignments he's got left to mark.

My triceps ache. It must be from helping Steve cut holes in the ice so we could set the net. He said nighttime is best for catching fish, since the fish don't see the net. I'm starting to understand that surviving in the North means finding ways to outsmart nature.

We used a *tuuk*, a long wooden stick with a sharp metal end, to cut through the ice. It's harder than it sounds, since the ice is, like, three feet deep. "You think this is thick," Tom told me when I complained. "It's nothing compared to how thick the ice was when my dad first took me fishing. Back then, the ice was at least five feet deep this time of year. You can thank global warming that we don't have to dig so deep anymore."

Lenny, who was about to take his turn, scowled. "Global warming," he muttered under his breath. "The rest of the world screws up and we pay the price. It's not right."

I passed Lenny the *tuuk*. "You blaming me for global warming?" I felt my ears grow hot. That always happens to me when I'm angry.

"I didn't say nothing about you," Lenny said, but when he started cutting really hard with the *tuuk*, I got the feeling he did hold me personally responsible.

When Lenny hit water, he leaned back and shouted, "Yes!" His face looked different—relaxed. Then he started chipping away at the ice, his arm moving like a jackhammer. "We need to make a hole that's about two feet wide," he said. "Get the clicker."

"What's a clicker?"

"It's a *nulujiutik*," Tom said.

"Thanks a lot," I told him. "That really helps."

Tom grinned. "Here," he said, "it's this." He showed me a bright orange wooden plank about four feet long and six inches wide.

"That thing's so bright it hurts my eyes," I told him.

"The color makes it easier to spot under the ice."

Tom turned the plank over. Underneath was a green wooden arm that swung up and down. "This clicker is one of our greatest inventions," Tom said. "When the plank floats underneath the ice, all you got to do is pull on this rope here." He pointed to a long length of rope attached to the green arm. "That brings the arm flush against the plank and pushes forward this little metal claw. The claw grabs the ice and propels the whole thing away from you."

Tom tapped his hand against a metal plate fastened to the underside of the plank. "The tapping on this metal plate makes the clicking sound," he explained.

"And you use that to set the fishing net?"

Tom raised his eyebrows. "It's hard to explain," he said. "You've got to see how it works."

I helped Tom tie a long line of rope onto the metal ring at the end of the clicker. Once Lenny's hole was big enough, we slid the clicker and the rope under the ice. Then we knotted the other end of the rope. It was tricky, but with three of us working together, it went okay.

"I'm gonna hold onto this end of the rope. You head out onto the ice and listen for the clicker," Tom told me. "It'll move under the ice as I pull the rope. With every pull, it'll go a little farther."

"Okay," I said, though I didn't really know what he meant. How was I supposed to hear something under all that ice?

I squatted on the ice, Inuit-style. Except for my own breathing and the *whoosh* of the wind, I couldn't hear a thing. Man, I thought, is it ever quiet up here!

I looked toward Tom and shrugged. He pointed to his ear. "Listen!" he said.

"I am listening!" I shouted back.

"You have to be patient," said Steve, who'd joined me on the ice. Patience has never been one of my better qualities.

Steve squatted next to me and lowered his head so his ear nearly brushed the ice. "Pull harder!" he shouted at Tom.

Steve raised one finger to his lips and gestured for me to lower my head to the ice too. When he raised his eyebrows, I knew he wanted to know whether I could hear the clicker.

I shook off the hood of my parka so I could hear better. The side of my head nearly grazed the ice, but I still couldn't hear any clicking. I turned to Steve and shook my head. "I've gotta go check on the dogs," he said. "Keep listening. Move around a little if you have to. It'll help you stay warm. This part can take a while."

By then, the sky was as black as Geraldine's braid. I shifted a little to the left, listening some more. Now I heard something, but it wasn't coming from underneath the ice. It sounded like "*whoo! whoo!*" and it was coming from the dark sky. Then something huge and white flapped its wings over my head. "Wow!" I said out loud, covering my mouth. If only my mom could have been there.

"What are you so excited about?" Lenny shouted once the bird was out of sight. "Never seen a snowy owl before?"

I couldn't tell him that for me, seeing that snowy owl and hearing his hoot felt almost like a sign, a message that I needed to be a little more patient. Maybe I didn't always take enough time to look or listen carefully enough.

I thought about that as I crawled along the ice, my head only a few inches from its surface. And then I heard it, a distant *click click* of metal under the ice. "I hear it!" I shouted. "Now what?"

That cracked Lenny and Tom up. "Now what?" Tom called out. "You keep listening! You're only about fifteen feet from the first hole, Noah. You've got a ways to go. The net's one-hundred-and-fifty freakin' feet long!"

We were out on the lake for another two hours. That's how long it took for me to follow the clicker and for the three of us to cut a second hole in the ice and pull the rope and the clicker up through it. It wasn't easy to hear the clicker, and we even started cutting out a hole that turned out to be in the wrong place. But once we had both ends of the rope, all we had to do was attach the net to one end and pull it out the other.

But at least the net is set. We are catching fish right now, while everyone except me is asleep. I have to admit that even with all that work, it's a good plan.

FIFTeen

Lenny's and Tom's voices wake me.

Lenny whistles as the two of them peek out through the crack in the tent door. "Look at her out there. Ain't she beautiful?" I figure they're talking about Geraldine. I think of her silky hair, and the way it sometimes looks navy blue. And I think of the way her dark eyes twinkle when she says something funny.

Tom is crouched on his knees next to Lenny. "She's beautiful all right. But cruel."

"Yeah," Lenny says, "she's going to give us some beating today, that's for sure."

Geraldine cruel? Geraldine beating up on us? I don't think so.

I sit up in my sleeping bag and rub the sleep from my eyes. The stove is making crackling sounds. "I have to take a leak," I say.

"You might change your mind when you see what's going on out there," Tom says.

I crawl out of my sleeping bag and over to where Tom and Lenny are. Tom makes room so I can see outside too. Only there isn't anything to see. Just white. Everywhere. That's when I understand what Tom and Lenny have been talking about. It's not Geraldine. It's not any girl at all. It's the weather. Beautiful and cruel.

"Is this a whiteout?" I ask the guys.

"Sure is," Tom says.

I still have to pee.

I pull on my parka and put on Dad's boots and my mitts. Even from inside the tent, we can hear the wind howling. I take a deep breath. This isn't going to be fun. When I crawl out from the tent, the wind smacks my face so hard I'm sure it'll leave a bruise.

Lenny pokes the top of his head out of the tent. "Hey, city boy, bring some wood when you're done taking your leak!" he shouts.

"Don't call me city boy!" I shout back, but I know there's no point. Lenny is already back inside. He'll never hear me over the wind.

The snow is coming down at a forty-five-degree angle. It isn't soft snow like the kind you see in movies or on Christmas cards. These are tiny sharp pellets that prick at my skin like needles. But there are so many of them and they are coming down so quickly, they seem to be making the whole world white.

I don't want to wander too far from the tent. I can't see more than a few inches in front of me, and it would be easy to get lost out here. But I also want to be sure the guys won't see me. I'll never hear the end of it if they catch me with my fly open.

I try heading out in a straight line. I watch for landmarks in case I have trouble finding my way back. I see two small bushes in a row, but then there are lots of small bushes. Then I spot a jerry can that has probably been used for siphoning gas into a snowmobile.

I continue a few more feet. Walking is easier if I keep my head down. Okay, I think, now's as good a time as any. I'll just get this over with, collect some wood and head back. Maybe Steve will say the conditions are too bad for us to empty the fishing net. I hope so, but I kind of doubt it. I remember something Dad told me about Steve: "He's lived here so long he thinks like an Inuk." I'm pretty sure stormy conditions—even a complete whiteout—can't stop the Inuit from catching fish. After all, we've got to eat, and so do the dogs.

It's so cold that at first I think I won't be able to pee. But once I start, I feel like I'll never be able to stop. I try to concentrate on the puff of smoke my pee makes as it hits the ground, not on how the cold is seeping inside my bones and how the wind is whipping my face and fingers.

I had to take off my mitts to unzip my fly and now my fingers are numb. I fumble as I zip up my pants. Thank god my dick didn't freeze right off.

The snow is coming down even harder now. I watch for the jerry can. Is that it? It seemed windy when I was walking away from the tent, but now that I'm headed back, the wind is twice as strong. It feels as if it might blow me right over. Small steps. I'll just take small steps. Rats! What I hoped was the jerry can turns out to be a branch.

That reminds me: I almost forgot to look for branches. Luckily, there are a few more under the bush. As I reach down to grab at them a gust of wind sweeps down and carries them away. I hear a crack as, somewhere close by, a branch breaks. But with all this snow, I can't tell where it lands.

What I'd give to be back in the warm tent. Even if Lenny's in it.

There it is—the jerry can. And there are branches too, lots of them. Quickly, I make a bundle. I know I'm not far from the tent now. I try imagining how good it'll feel to warm my hands in front of the stove. And do I smell pancakes? I've been so busy fighting the elements I didn't realize how hungry I am. I hope Steve has syrup in one of his boxes.

Just then, I hear steps—heavy ones—coming toward me. "Who is it?" I call out. I stretch the top of my hands out in front of me like a blind man groping in the dark, which, in a way, I am.

The only answer I get is the cracking sound as another branch breaks. "Who is it?" I hear the fear in my voice. If there's a polar bear out here, I tell myself, I'd have seen tracks. Or would the snow, falling so quickly, have covered them?

The steps are coming closer.

My breathing speeds up, and the top of my chest starts to hurt. I can't tell if it's from the cold or from fear. Probably both.

"Hey."

I recognize the husky voice.

"Geraldine," I say. "What are you doing out here?"

I can see her now. She's got on an old-fashioned pair of snowshoes, the kind made from wood and rawhide. They explain the heavy steps I just heard.

"Did I scare you?" she asks. Her dark eyes twinkle.

"Nah," I say. I'm pretty sure she can tell I'm lying.

"Steve said he'd make pancakes for breakfast," she says. "Me and my *ataata* are invited too. After that, we're going to empty the nets. All of us."

"All of us?"

Geraldine laughs. I figure that means me too.

sixteen

Steve makes the best pancakes ever. They're not too thin, not too thick. Plus they're sweet and salty at the same time. And there's pure maple syrup, not the fake kind. Since there aren't any maple trees up here, I figure Steve must've brought the syrup back with him from one of his trips south. He's from Thunder Bay, Ontario, and his parents still live there. I wonder if it's weird for them that he lives up here and that their grandchildren speak Inuktitut.

I pass Steve my tin plate for a third helping. "These pancakes are amazing."

Steve points to a cardboard box on the floor. "That's my secret recipe. Store-bought pancake mix from the Northern. Low fat, low salt."

When I get back to Montreal, I'll put that on the shopping list. Only maybe pancakes taste better when you're winter camping and the polar bear you've been afraid of turns out to be a pretty girl on snowshoes.

"Eat up, everyone. We're going to need all our strength to empty those nets," Steve says, rubbing his hands together. "Something tells me they're gonna be loaded with Arctic char."

"I wanna help too!" Etua says. He's jumping up and down again.

"I don't think so." Steve bends down and looks into Etua's eyes so he'll understand he's serious. "The weather's too bad out there for a little guy like you."

Etua pouts. "I'm not a little guy. I'm Spiderman!"

"Spiders don't like the snow. It's bad for their webs," I tell him.

Etua nods. That makes sense to him at least. I sure wish I could trade places with Etua and stay inside the tent doing puzzles. Joseph gets to stay inside too, to look after Etua. When I offer to take Joseph's place, Steve says he doesn't think it would be a good idea. "Thanks for offering, but whoever stays in the tent needs to know how woodstoves work," he tells me. "These things can be pretty dangerous."

When the rest of us head out after breakfast, we keep close. Along our way, we pass the dogs. Steve and Joseph and Jakopie have tied the teams up in a clearing at the edge of the camp. The dogs are staked out at regular intervals on a long cable strung up between two spruce trees. Each dog is tied to the cable at intervals of about six feet, by a smaller cable that hooks onto his collar. The dogs can only get close enough to touch noses.

"How come you don't let them huddle together to stay warm?" I ask Steve.

"That'd never work," he tells me. "They'd fight or get tangled up. But don't worry about the dogs, Noah. They were made for this kind of weather."

I make a point of walking behind Tom and Lenny to give myself a little extra protection from the wind. If the weather were a girl, the way Tom and Lenny talked about her this morning, she was in some bad mood.

"You think this is gusty?" Geraldine's father says with a laugh. His face is rounder than Geraldine's. "This is nothing compared to when I was a kid hunting seals with my *ataata*. Oh, those were gusty days all right. Much gustier than today." It's the first thing he's said all morning.

The Inuit may be people of few words, but Matthew, Geraldine's father, is quieter than the rest. Quieter even than Jakopie. Still, I get the feeling Matthew is the sort of person who enjoys watching life happen around him. And fishing. Geraldine told me fishing is her dad's favorite thing. "He says it gives him time to think," she said.

Matthew and Geraldine head for their own fishing spot a little farther out on the lake. Roy goes to give them a hand with their net.

This morning, there is no time for the kind of thinking Matthew likes to do. Not with our net full of Arctic char, some already dead, but most wriggling for dear life, their silver bodies glimmering against the snow. Steve was right. The net is so heavy it takes four of us to pull it out from under the ice.

Tom is standing closest to the hole, where the ice is slick. As we pull, water gushes out and freezes up almost as soon as it makes contact with the air. When the net is nearly out, Tom loses his footing and falls over on the ice.

Tom takes Lenny with him when he falls. That leaves Steve and me holding the rope. And since the net is too heavy for just the two of us, we end up letting go. Luckily, Etua isn't around to hear his dad swear. When Tom and Lenny are back on their feet, we start over again. Steve grits his teeth as we pull. My back is killing me.

Because of the way the snow is coming down, we can't see Geraldine and her dad and Roy.

It doesn't take as long this time to get the net back on the ice. I tug so hard I forget how cold I am and how the wind is stinging my face.

"Good work, guys!" Steve is saying. "Look at all these fish. There's plenty for us and for the dogs too."

This time when Tom collapses on the ice he does it on purpose. "Nothing tastes as good as fresh-caught Arctic char," he says, stretching his legs out in front of him so he looks like one of those Russian dancers.

Lenny rubs his belly. "Fresh-caught Arctic char tastes even better than ptarmigan liver," he says. His eyes are shining, and I know he's watching for my reaction.

Somewhere in the distance, we hear a loud cracking noise. It startles me. "Was that thunder?" I ask Steve.

"We never get thunder during snowstorms. Must be the ice cracking somewhere out on the lake."

"Or Kajutaijug!" Lenny says, cackling. "Maybe she wants to show us her titties."

I don't think that's especially funny, but I'm way too tired to tell Lenny so. So I laugh instead. Another gust of wind hits me and nearly takes my ski tuque with it.

"Hey, look at that!" Tom points up at the sky. Somehow, when we were too busy to notice, the bottom of the sky has turned from gray to pink.

I'm reaching into my parka for my camera when Steve taps my shoulder. "Let's head back to the tent. Right now. These winds must be gusting at ninety kilometers an hour. We'll come back later when it's calmer and when the visibility's better."

"What about the fish?" Lenny asks. "You don't want the polar bears to get 'em."

"We'll worry about the fish later."

"We should take some of the fish with us," Lenny says.

"Let's go," Steve says. "Now!" It's the same tone he used before with Etua.

"Roy! Geraldine! Matthew!" Steve shouts as we make our way back to the tents. It's almost impossible to see now. I can tell from the tension in Steve's voice he's worried about the others. "Can you hear me?" he shouts. The five of us are walking so close together now it's like we're one person.

The fact that Steve is worried makes me worry too. "Geraldine!" I shout.

Lenny makes a guffawing sound. "You got a thing for Geraldine?" he asks.

"No," I say, a little too quickly.

"Guess you'd like to see her titties, wouldn't you?"

My ears get very, very hot.

Before I can think about whether what I'm about to do is a good idea, I punch Lenny. Right in the mouth. I do it for Geraldine and for all the girls I know, like Tammy Akerman and Chris L'Ecuyer's little sister, Irene. Mostly, though, I do it for me.

For a second or two, Lenny just looks surprised. "What'd you do that for?' he asks, rubbing his lips. But then his eyes narrow, and I'm pretty sure he's about to hit me back, probably a lot harder than I hit him.

But Steve pulls Lenny away. "Break it up, guys," he says. "Right now."

Lenny drops his arm to his side. I imagine he's making a fist, though I can't tell for sure because he's got mitts on.

"Sure thing," Lenny tells Steve.

Lenny inches a little closer to me. He's smirking again. "Later," he whispers into my ear.

I can feel my heart pounding in my ears. I shouldn't have started up with Lenny, but he shouldn't have said that about Geraldine.

"Roy! Geraldine! Matthew!" Steve calls again.

In the distance, we hear the dogs barking. They can probably tell too, that Steve is upset.

Up ahead, where the tents are, we can just make out a small dark figure.

"Etua!" Steve shouts as he runs toward the tent. "What's wrong with you? I told you to stay inside! Where's Joseph?"

The three of us are running too. Etua is jumping up and down again, only now he's crying too. "Hurry, *Ataata!*" Etua manages to say between sobs.

"What happened?" Steve asks.

Etua's eyes are wet with tears. "It's Joseph! He cut his thumb off! Oh, *Ataata*, there's blood everywhere!"

seventeen

The outside of Steve and Etua's tent looks like a crime scene. Etua is right—there's blood everywhere. Inside too. On the floor, on the walls, even on the stove door. Later, I wonder how the blood managed to splatter so far.

Joseph is sitting on the floor of the tent, rocking back and forth and moaning when we come in. His eyes are glazed over, just like Tarksalik's were after the accident. Joseph nods when he sees Steve, but then, a second later, his head sinks to his chest and he passes out.

That makes Etua sob even harder. "Joseph's dead! Dead!" he cries. "It's because of me! I told him we needed more wood for the stove. And now he's dead!"

Steve is crouched on the floor next to Joseph. "He isn't dead, Etua. He's in shock. He's lost a lot of blood, but he's not dead. Look at his chest! You can see him breathing!"

Etua chokes on his tears. "Are you sure, *Ataata*?"

We have to stop the bleeding. Even I know that. "What can we do?" I ask Steve. Tom, Lenny and Jakopie are standing next to me, ready to pitch in. Geraldine, Roy and Matthew have shown up too, probably alerted by Etua's wailing.

Steve barks out orders. "One of you get the first-aid kit! Someone else get towels! You'll need to cut them into strips. And get me the satellite phone—quick! Matthew, I'm gonna need your snowmobile to get Joseph back to George River. Can you clear it off for me? Two of you had better go do it. It'll be safer."

"I'm not sure you should be traveling in this kind of weather," Matthew says.

"We don't have a choice," Steve tells him. "Go clear it off."

Since I know where the satellite phone is, I get it from Steve's backpack by the tent door. There's blood on the backpack too. After Joseph injured himself, he must have stumbled into the tent, probably to look for a towel to help stop the bleeding.

I'm squatting on the ground, rifling through the backpack, when I happen to turn my head and look outside through the crack in the tent. That's when I spot it—Joseph's thumb, covered by a thin, thin layer of snow. Seeing it gives me that same lurching feeling in my stomach. It's fat and flesh-colored; the nail at the top is thick and gnarled-looking. The thumb is lying under a spruce bough next to Steve's ax, the one Joseph was using to cut logs for the fire.

I have to tell the others. Can't doctors reattach body parts like thumbs? Only where are we going to find a doctor?

I suck in my breath to steady myself. "Uh, Steve," I say, trying to keep my voice level, "Joseph's thumb's out there, on the ground."

"Go get it," Steve calls out as if he's talking about a log for the fire. "Someone's gonna have to sew that thumb back on. Etua, get Noah some snow to keep Joseph's thumb cold."

Eating ptarmigan liver is nothing compared to picking up someone's thumb from the snow. I'm afraid I'll puke again, but thank god I don't. It's a big thumb, nearly a third the size of my palm, and even though it's been out in the snow, it's still slightly warm. Is it my imagination, or can I feel it pulse inside my hand, almost as if the thumb has a heartbeat? I carry the thumb back into the tent.

"We've got to stop the bleeding," Steve is saying. "Joseph, can you hear me?"

Tom and Jakopie have found towels, and Geraldine is cutting them into strips. I think about telling her to be careful, but I don't. I don't want to do anything that might set Lenny off again.

Steve has wrapped one strip of toweling around Joseph's hand, but the blood is seeping through like a red river. Again, I think of Tarksalik and the pool of blood and how she managed to drag herself to the side of the road. Joseph's blood is the same color as Tarksalik's.

"I've never seen so much blood!" Geraldine says softly as she hands Steve another strip of towel.

"We've got to make a tourniquet—fast," Steve says. "And we need to keep his hand elevated so it's over his heart. That'll reduce the flow of blood." Geraldine helps Steve make the tourniquet. Then she and Steve use another piece of towel to make a sling that will keep Joseph's hand higher than his heart.

Etua is back with the snow. "I need some strips of towel too," I tell him. "To wrap the thumb in." In a way, it's a relief to wrap Joseph's thumb inside the towel. I pack it in as much snow as I can. At least this way, I won't have to keep looking at the thumb or feel its strange pulse inside my palm.

Lenny grabs the satellite phone. "Do I phone Mathilde? Is that what you want me to do? What's the number at the clinic?"

"Three, three, seven..." Lenny dials as Steve calls out the number. I hope Mathilde answers.

The phone makes a buzzing sound as it rings and rings. No one's there.

"Now what?" Lenny asks.

"Try my dad's. Maybe she's at his place." Only I don't know Dad's number. When I'm in Montreal, he's always the one who phones me. Every Sunday at exactly 11:00 AM. He's never missed a Sunday since he moved to Nunavik.

"I know the number," Tom says, and he tells it to Lenny. Tom must notice me looking at him. "I call him once in a while," he explains. "When there's trouble at home," he adds, lowering his voice.

I'm glad to hear Dad's voice on the other end through the crackling sounds of static. Even if Mathilde isn't there, he'll know where to find her.

"Good to hear from you, Lenny Etok," I hear Dad say. "I've been worrying about you guys. I'm watching the weather on the net and listening to the FM. It looks pretty bad up where you are. Gale-force winds. It's way calmer down here. Minus seventeen right now, but hardly any wind at all. So tell me, how's my boy doing?"

"Uh, look, Bill," Lenny says, stumbling for words, "I'm not calling about the weather. We got a bit of a problem. Is Mathilde around?"

I hear Dad suck in his breath. "I'll put her right on."

Lenny passes Steve the phone. Steve gestures for Lenny to come and press down on the toweling on Joseph's hand. "Hey, Mathilde," Steve says, cradling the phone under his chin, "Joseph's cut his thumb clean off. It's bleeding pretty bad. He's in and out of consciousness. We've made a tourniquet and we're keeping the hand elevated. But you're gonna have to tell me what to do next."

It's hard to make out exactly what Mathilde is saying since she isn't a loud talker the way Dad is. But I can tell from the steady rhythm of her voice she is giving Steve instructions. Steve listens and nods. Then he catches Lenny's eye and raises one hand in the air. "Raise his hand even higher," Steve whispers. "That'll help with the bleeding." Steve nods again in response to something else Mathilde says. "Yes, we've got the thumb," he tells her. "Noah found it. Okay, I got that. We can't let the thumb freeze."

But even with Joseph's hand elevated, the bleeding doesn't let up. Joseph opens his eyes and moans as he looks around the tent. His eyes land on the blood splattered on the stove door. "I'm sorry," he whispers. "I didn't mean to cause any tr—" But he passes out again before he can finish his sentence.

eIGHTeen

Mathilde says we'll need a surgeon to reattach Joseph's thumb. If it wasn't so stormy up here, she'd try to arrange for a medevac plane to come out to Short Lake. But in conditions like these, it makes the most sense for Steve to try and get Joseph back to town. There's a flight scheduled to leave for Kuujjuaq this afternoon. If the sky stays clear in George River and the winds don't pick up too much—and if Steve can make it to George River in time—they can get Joseph on the plane. Mathilde will call ahead to the Kuujjuaq hospital so they'll be ready to operate as soon as Joseph arrives.

It sounds like a good plan, but of course it depends on a lot of things going right. I pack Joseph's thumb in a plastic bag that's half-full of snow. The bag goes into a cooler that Tom helps me strap down to the back of Matthew's snowmobile. We also pack water, food, a portable stove, tarps, a pup tent and the satellite phone. If all goes well, the trip should take about two hours by snowmobile, but if anything goes wrong, Steve and Joseph will need emergency supplies.

"We'll be fine," Steve keeps saying when we tell him what we've packed. But the way he repeats himself makes me think he's worried too.

Matthew offers to come along, but in the end, he and Steve figure the extra weight on the snowmobile will only slow things down. "Besides," Steve tells Matthew as the rest of us gather to see Steve and Joseph off, "I'm going to need you to keep an eye on these guys. And I don't just mean Spiderman here." Steve leans over to hug Etua. Then he turns to Lenny and me. "You two behave yourselves, okay?"

I nod my head.

"Sure thing, man," Lenny mutters.

Joseph lifts his good hand to wave good-bye. He's too weak to speak. I sure hope Steve can get him on that plane to Kuujjuaq and that the plane won't be grounded. The snow is still coming down hard, and the wind is as strong as it was when I got up.

Steve and Joseph are headed into the wind. Steve lowers his face as he turns the key in the ignition. Then he presses down with his thumb on the throttle and the two of them take off.

When Etua squeezes my hand, I squeeze his back. I'm supposed to be looking after him, but in a weird way, being responsible for him makes me feel a little better too.

At first, Matthew doesn't say a thing as the snowmobile heads away from the camp. But once the buzzing sound of the motor fades, he turns to face us. When he speaks, his voice is quiet, calm. "We're going to need to empty those nets and feed the dogs," he says. "It makes the most sense for us to work together as a group. But let's clean up first. The sooner we get rid of the smell of blood, the better."

We hear a thud, followed by an echo that is almost as loud. Somewhere not too far from us, another heavy branch must have fallen to the ground. My shoulders tense up.

Am I the only one thinking about Kajutaijug?

Because Etua is getting tired of hanging out in the tent— even after we've washed away all the blood—we decide to let him come out to the lake with the rest of us. "Just as long as someone keeps an eye on him," Matthew says.

"No problem," I say.

"Sure thing," Tom adds.

Geraldine and Lenny raise their eyebrows.

Etua knows more about net fishing than I do. A bit of net is still caught under the ice, and when we lift it out, we find more fish. When we turn the net over on the ice, some of the fish are still thrashing from side to side as if they're trying to swim.

Etua uses a short heavy stick to kill them. One swift whack to the head, and the fish stop moving altogether. Etua laughs as he whacks the fish.

If someone had told me two weeks ago, when I was still in Montreal, that today I'd be watching a laughing five-year-old clubbing fish to death, I'd have been disgusted. But now that I'm up here, things look different. We need to eat, the dogs need to eat, and there's no point making the fish suffer any more than they have to. It's better to kill them quickly than to let them suffocate on the ice.

That gets me thinking about how the kids at school— even Geraldine—were surprised when we didn't put Tarksalik down. With all the snow, it's impossible to see the dogs, but I know from the occasional yelp that they're still out there, ready to get back to work when it comes time to bring us home.

For the Inuit, dogs aren't pets the way they are for us in the city. Maybe *we're* the weird ones—keeping dogs on leashes, taking them for walks in the park and training them to sit or shake a paw. Until now, I never gave much thought to how we treat animals in the city.

Once all the fish are dead, we pile them onto the back of the *qamutik*. Most are already half-frozen. "When we get 'em back to the camp, we'll lay them out in rows so they can freeze through," Tom says. The wind whips the wool pompom hanging from the woolen string on top of his *nassak*, so the pompom lands on his forehead, just over his nose. Tom shakes it off his face. "Once we're back in George River," he says, "Steve'll bag the fish and Joseph… er…" Tom catches himself. "Maybe not Joseph. Not for a while, anyhow."

"D'you think he'll be able to carve again?" I ask Tom. Dad told me Joseph is one of the best carvers in all Nunavik.

"I hope so," Tom says. "Joseph sells his stuff to some fancy art gallery in Quebec City. That helps pay for dog food."

Geraldine and her dad are helping us load fish too. "No sense in worrying about Joseph," Matthew says. He looks out at the snow and then up at the sky. "What happens now ain't up to us. Joseph's in bigger hands."

Afterward, we all go to the Snowflakes' spot on the lake and load up their fish. Etua brings his stick, but he doesn't have much work since most of the Snowflakes' fish are already dead.

My elbow rubs against Geraldine's as I reach down for another armful of fish. She is humming a tune I don't recognize. She could move away, but she doesn't. I figure it's a sign that maybe she likes me. At least I hope it is.

"Hey, Noah," Lenny calls from out on the ice. It's hard to know how far away he is exactly because of the way the snow is blowing. "Come give me a hand, will ya?" Maybe because it's the first time he's called me Noah, I stop what I'm doing and head over. Geraldine is still humming.

I see Lenny's dark eyes shining even through all the snow. It looks as if he is only about twenty feet away from me now. When I come closer, I can hear him chuckle. "Hey, Noah, have a look over here." He is pointing at something on the ice. His lip is swollen from where I punched him.

The fact that he uses my name twice in a row should tell me Lenny is up to something. But I don't figure that out at first.

I move toward him, but a fresh gust of wind blows in and for a few seconds all I see is snow. I can still hear Lenny chuckling, but the sound seems to be getting more distant. The snow is swirling all over. I put my arms out in front of me. I don't want to bump into Lenny.

When the wind dies down, and I get to where Lenny was, he isn't there. What's going on?

"Lenny!" I shout.

At first, he doesn't answer, but then I hear him. Only now his voice seems to be coming from a different direction altogether. "Over here, Noah," I hear him call out. "Hurry, will ya?"

I must have lost my sense of direction in that last whiteout. "I'm coming," I call as I turn around.

Again, I follow Lenny's voice, but when I get there, he is gone.

"Come on, Lenny!" This must be his idea of a joke.

Though I can't see him, it's as if I can feel his presence.

I turn to see whether he could be behind me. What if he jumps me? Worse still, what if he wants to beat the crap out of me? He must want to get back at me for punching him.

"Noah?" This time, Lenny's voice sounds really close. Is he going to disappear again?

Then, just like that, before I know what is happening, Lenny is beside me, pinning my arms behind my back. It's like he appeared out of nowhere. My heart is racing. With all the snow, the others won't know what he's about to do to me.

I'm so afraid I nearly lose my breath. I gulp for air and try kicking him in the leg, but my boots are too big and Lenny sidesteps away just in time. He's laughing, but I still don't trust him.

I feel the heat from Lenny's lips near my right ear. He won't let go of my elbows. The weird thing is, he's not hurting me.

Lenny leans in even closer. I still want to break away from him, but it's like I don't have any strength. Even if he isn't hurting me, I'm afraid he might.

I think of my dream about Roland Ipkins. Now Lenny spins me around so we're facing each other. I don't want to look into his eyes, but I've got no choice.

Lenny has that smirk on his face, but his eyes don't look angry. Is this another one of his tricks?

"You afraid of me?" he asks.

There doesn't seem to be any point in lying. "Uh... yeah," I tell him.

Lenny loosens his grip on my elbows. "Guess you forgot what my great-uncle Charlie Etok said about fear the other night: it tires you out worse than anything else."

I shake my elbows loose. "Guess I did."

"There's one more thing I want to know. How come you wear such a silly hat anyway?"

"It's a ski tu—" But before I'm done my sentence, Lenny whips the ski tuque off my head. It flutters in the wind like a flag.

"Give it back!" I cry out.

Lenny just laughs and tosses my tuque into the air. I guess I should be happy he isn't beating me to a pulp. Still, my ears are burning from the cold. I cover my ears with my hands. "C'mon, Lenny!"

"Would the two of you quit fooling around and get back to work?" It's Matthew. He's got my tuque in his hands. He throws it over to me.

Geraldine is coming this way too. Her mouth is open, and at first I think it's because she's singing. Then I realize she isn't singing; she's shouting. At first, I can't make out what she's saying because of the wind. But I can see her lips moving. And then, when she gets a little closer, I hear the words too. They are so high-pitched, you'd think they could travel all the way back to George River.

"Where's Etua?" she yells.

That's when the dogs start barking too.

I look over to where Etua was inspecting the fish, checking whether they were really dead. There's no sign of him.

nineteen

"Etua!" Geraldine shouts. "Where are you? Etua!" Geraldine's dark eyes have a wild look. "He was right n-next to me," she says, her voice breaking. "Then I turned around and he was gone. Etua!"

The rest of us are shouting too. "Spiderman!" I call, thinking maybe he'll hear that better than just his name. But when we stop to listen for him, all we hear is the wind's fierce whistle, the dogs' barking and our own frightened-sounding echoes.

"He can't be far," Matthew is saying. His voice still sounds calm. He raises one hand over his eyes to help him see better.

"Then why isn't he answering?" Geraldine sounds like she's about to cry.

"Maybe he can't hear us over the wind and the dogs," I say. "I couldn't hear you before, and you were screaming."

I'm chewing on the inside of my lip. I bite down so hard, I taste blood.

I shouldn't have gone out onto the lake when Lenny called me. I should've thought about Etua. I promised to keep an eye on him. I screwed up. Again.

"We should split up into three search parties," Tom says. Nobody argues. Not even Matthew.

"Jakopie, Roy and I'll head into the bush. Matthew and Geraldine, check the tents. You two cover the lake," Tom tells Lenny and me. I don't complain about being stuck with Lenny. The only thing that matters now is finding Etua.

The lake looks bigger and snowier than ever. Is Etua out there somewhere? I feel inside my pocket for the ptarmigan feather Tom gave me. At first, I can't find it, but then I feel something thin and hard way at the bottom of my pocket, where the lint collects. Yes, that's it. I must be getting desperate if I'm starting to believe in lucky feathers.

"We'd better find him soon," Geraldine whispers, and now I can tell she's really having trouble fighting the tears. "He could freeze to death out here."

I pat Geraldine's elbow. "We'll find him."

"Etua! Spiderman!" I shout as Lenny and I trudge along the ice.

"Etua! Spiderman!" a voice echoes back. This time, it isn't my voice echoing. It's Geraldine's. She's out there calling for Etua too.

I keep my eyes on the snow near my feet. Maybe we'll see small tracks. Maybe Etua fell and he's having trouble getting up. His parka probably weighs more than he does.

But with the snow coming down so hard, Etua's tracks will be covered in no time, and so will Etua.

"He's wearing a red parka," I say to Lenny. "And a red *nassak*."

"I know," Lenny snaps. You'd think I'd said something really annoying. I shouldn't let it bother me, but it does. Again, I think of Roland Ipkins. I remember the anti-bullying workshops we had in elementary school. The lady who came to talk to our class told us we should feel sorry for bullies. At the time, I thought she was out of her mind. Imagine feeling sorry for Roland Ipkins, who used to squash my sandwiches at lunch and once put dog shit in my rain boots. There was no way I could feel sorry for him! But I'm beginning to wonder if maybe Lenny isn't a bully after all. At least not the kind of bully I'm used to. Maybe Lenny is more into tricks than torture. Maybe kids up north don't just have a different attitude to animals; maybe kids up here also have a different attitude to other kids. Maybe they're not mean the way city kids can be.

Lenny stops for a few seconds to look out at the lake like Matthew did, using his hand for a visor. "You shouldn't have left him alone," Lenny mutters. There he goes again, criticizing me. And I'm not just going to keep taking it. Just like I shouldn't have kept taking it from Roland Ipkins all through elementary school and then into high school.

"You shouldn't have called me over and tried to trick me," I say. "And you shouldn't have taken my ski tuque."

"Who started it?" Lenny says. "Who punched me in the face?"

"You started it. You've been ragging on me since I got here."

Lenny doesn't have anything to say to that.

I'm not done yet. "We all said we'd watch Etua. Not just me."

Lenny doesn't have anything to say to that, either.

We trudge a little farther. Lenny is breathing hard. Or is it me? The wind burns my face, and my lips are so chapped they hurt.

I think of Steve and Joseph out on the snowmobile in this storm. Will they make it back to town in time for Joseph to catch the plane to Kuujjuaq?

Then I remember Joseph's thumb on the snow outside the tent and Tarksalik lying on the road in a pool of blood. And now Etua is missing. People, even grown people, die in weather like this. How's a little kid going to make it?

It's starting to feel like the whole world is falling apart around me. I'm not angry the way I was a few minutes ago; now I'm more sad than anything else. And hopeless.

"Steve'll never forgive us if something bad happens to Etua," I say. I am talking more to myself than to Lenny.

Lenny stops in his tracks. When he raises one hand in the air, I feel the muscles in my back and stomach contract. I'm wondering if now is when he's going to punch me or maybe strangle me instead. When Lenny puts his hand on my shoulder, I feel relieved, but still a little nervous. I can't trust him. He doesn't like me any more than I like him. Probably less.

"Will you cut it out?" Lenny says, looking me hard in the eye. "Nothing bad's gonna happen to Etua."

I shake my head, but I don't say what I'm thinking, which is: How do you know? And if you're so sure and so big and tough, how come your hand is shaking?

"Etua! Spiderman! Where are you?" Lenny is shouting now. We're walking again, side by side, not saying a word except to call for Etua.

"What's that?" I say, pointing to a spot of color on the shore about thirty feet from where we are, though it's hard to judge distances with the snow blowing so hard.

"I don't see nothin'," Lenny says.

You mean *anything*. You don't see anything, I think. Something tells me Lenny wouldn't appreciate a grammar lesson right now.

I tug on Lenny's arm. "I see something." My chest starts to feel a little lighter. It hasn't been long since Etua went missing. If we find him now, he should be fine. "Maybe it's Etua."

We pick up our speed. "Do you see it now?" I ask Lenny.

"I see somethin'," he says. "But it's not red."

We are walking against the wind. But I don't care about the snow or the cold or the wind. I don't even care about whether Lenny plans to try and kill me.

Lenny's right. Whatever we've spotted isn't red, so it can't be Etua. The heavy feeling in my chest comes back. Maybe we shouldn't have bothered heading to the shore. Maybe if we'd kept walking straight out on the lake, we'd have found Etua by now. Maybe we should turn back right now.

I don't realize I'm talking out loud.

Lenny grabs my elbow. "Can you quit saying 'maybe' all the time?" he says. "You're driving me nuts. But I'll tell you one thing: Etua shouldn't have gone off by himself. What was he thinking?" Lenny releases his grip.

"He's just a kid."

"A dumb kid. Can you believe he thinks he's Spiderman?"

I don't like Lenny calling Etua dumb. "He's got an imagination. Usually, that's a good thing."

"Not if it gets you lost in a whiteout, it isn't."

I try imagining what might have made Etua wander off without telling any of us where he was going. "Maybe Etua was thinking like Spiderman," I say, thinking out loud. "Maybe he was trying to save somebody."

Lenny groans. "Now what are you going on about? You sound like an old lady."

I decide to ignore him. "I'm just thinking maybe Etua had a reason for taking off the way he did."

We're getting quite close to whatever it was we saw from out on the lake.

"Looks like some branches that musta got loose from a snare trap," Lenny says. "But it's not Etua."

I'm not so sure. If Etua thinks he's Spiderman, maybe he saw—or heard—something out here he thought needed saving.

"Spiderman!" I shout. My voice is getting hoarse.

"Spiderman!" Lenny joins in.

The snare trap is only a few feet behind the branches. It's a wire noose attached to a small stump with some greenery around the wire. The trap is empty.

"See that?" Lenny says, leaning down to inspect it. "It's got fur on it. Over here. Looks like there was something in this trap not too long ago."

"Spiderman!" I call again.

I think I hear rustling in the low brush up ahead, so I head there. But Lenny pulls me back. When I turn to look at him, he's holding his index finger to his lips, leaning forward. He's listening, straining to hear sounds my own ears aren't trained to pick up.

Could be a bear. Lenny mouths the words.

At first, I think he's kidding. I know he'd enjoy seeing me panic. But Lenny's not smirking, and when he looks up at me, his pupils look really big. That's how I can tell he's scared.

So am I. The panicky feeling I had when I heard those heavy steps—that turned out to be Geraldine on snowshoes—and when I thought Lenny was going to beat the crap out of me comes back. Polar bears aren't like the ones you see in the Coke ads. They don't wave or smile when they see you coming. They hunt and stalk their prey. Sometimes for days in a row, waiting till the time is right to attack. I know because I've seen them do it on the Discovery Channel.

What if Lenny is right and there's a polar bear out there? What if he's been stalking us since we arrived at

Short Lake? And what if Etua is out there too? My whole body shivers, and this time it isn't because of the cold.

Lenny is Inuit. He's lived here all his life. He'll know what to do. I look at him and mouth the word *Etua*.

Lenny raises his hands to chest level, then lowers them slowly, as if he's pressing down on the keys of an imaginary piano. I know that means there's only one thing to do: wait.

I've never been much good at waiting. In Montreal, when there's a line at the store or the bank machine, I usually take off. I've got better things to do than stand around staring into space. I like to think of myself as a man of action.

Lenny closes his eyes, which strikes me as a weird thing to do. Now he's rocking back and forth on the balls of his feet. What in the world is he doing—going into some kind of trance? If I were a polar bear, I'd go after Lenny first. The thought makes me feel a little better. Lenny's big. He'd make a square meal even for a polar bear. Unless it was a really hungry polar bear. One who hadn't caught a seal recently. In that case, Lenny might just be an appetizer.

I have to fight an overwhelming urge to scream. I know I can't. The last thing you want to do when a polar bear is around is draw attention to yourself. But inside my head, I'm screaming.

Lenny opens his eyes and leans forward again. I can tell he's still listening. I try listening too, tuning in the way Lenny is doing.

All I can hear is the wind, and the soft *ping* the snow makes as it lands on the ground. And now I hear the rustling sounds again. Only now, those sounds are getting farther away. Is it a polar bear?

When Lenny sees me open my mouth, he shakes his head. I'm going to have to wait some more.

The first noise that comes out of Lenny is a sigh. A long, deep sigh. That must mean the coast is clear. "D'you really think it was a polar bear?" I whisper.

"I think I heard him breathing. But he's gone now."

"Do you think it's safe to start calling Etua again?"

"Soon," Lenny says.

In the end, though, we don't have to call for Etua. Because just after we turn to head back out onto the lake, Etua walks up to us as if he was there all along. "Etua!" Lenny and I cry out at once.

"Hi, Noah. Hi, Lenny," he says as if he has no idea we've been searching for him.

The fur collar on Etua's red parka is covered with snow, and his cheeks are as red as the parka. He's carrying something he holds out to show us. At first, I think it's a stuffed animal or a baby in a fur coat. Of course that makes no sense. A baby in a fur coat?

It's an animal, just not a stuffed one. It's an Arctic hare. A small dead white Arctic hare with black ear tips and strong sharp claws, freshly caught in the trap we spotted. Etua must have pried him loose. He probably shouldn't have done that. The hare must belong to whoever set the trap.

"I heard a squeaking noise," Etua says. "I thought someone needed me. But it was just a hare. He squeaked when he got caught in the trap."

"You shouldn't have gone off without telling us," I say.

"Especially not in weather like this," Lenny adds.

Etua isn't paying any attention. He's pulled back one of the hare's furry white front paws—as if the hare is a hand puppet—and is waving it at us.

Part of me wants to throttle him. He gave all of us a bad scare, and he almost made Geraldine cry. But he's back now, and there's something about the sight of that dead hare waving its paw that cracks me up. I laugh so hard my side hurts.

TWENTY

The trap belongs to Matthew. He has two more snare traps and a couple of leg-hold traps set up in different spots around the lake. The leg-hold traps are all metal; they are meant for catching foxes. The Inuit don't like to shoot foxes because bullet holes spoil the fur.

So Etua has to surrender his new toy. He doesn't want to. But Etua also knows we're upset with him for taking off, so he must sense it's not a good time to argue. "Okay," he says as he hands over the limp animal, waving its front paw one last time.

I watch later as Matthew skins the rabbit. He makes a slit under the rabbit's bum, then pulls the skin off like it's a glove.

Matthew hands the pelt to Geraldine. "It's pretty, but not as valuable as fox," she explains to me, running her fingers through the silky fur. "Now we keep most of the fox fur to make trim for parkas. But in the old days, we traded our fox fur with the *Qallunaat* for food and rifles. Those *Qallunaat* sure ripped us off," Geraldine says. Then she blushes. "Sorry," she says, "I didn't mean you."

"I don't mind if you call me a *Qallunaaq*," I tell her. "That's what I am. A white guy."

"I don't think of you like that." I can tell Geraldine is embarrassed from the way she's holding her head a little to the side.

"You don't?"

She blushes again.

"So how *do* you think of me?"

Geraldine pauses for a moment. "As Noah. Just Noah."

I figure that's a start. A good start.

We lay out the fish so they can freeze through. That'll make it easier to load them up when it's time to go back to George River.

We make a point of not storing the fish too close to the tents. Lenny and I told Matthew how we thought we heard a polar bear when we were searching for Etua. "If there's one out there," Matthew said, looking at the lake, "I'd rather let him have our fish than us."

Lenny is playing with the trigger on his rifle. Something tells me he'd like to shoot a polar bear.

Jakopie is hauling a block of ice up from the river. It's so big his arms barely reach around it.

"Need some help?" I ask him.

"Nah," he grunts.

"What's he need ice for anyhow?" I ask Tom.

"For making ice water."

"Didn't we bring drinking water with us?"

Jakopie turns to answer my question. "That's tap water. I can't stand the taste. It's not real water." I wonder what Jakopie would think of all the bottled water they sell in the grocery stores in Montreal. Probably not much.

We eat fried Arctic char for supper in the Snowflakes' tent. Everyone's there—Tom, Lenny, Jakopie, Etua, Roy and me. There's no shortage of fish. It's the first time I've ever tasted fresh-caught Arctic char. The flesh is peach-colored and it has a gamey, almost sweet taste. The crispy skin is good too. Geraldine and her dad rubbed the outside of the fish with salt before they put it on the stove.

Geraldine sprinkles more salt on her fish.

"I hope you get a discount at the Northern," I tell her. "You must go through a lot of salt."

Geraldine covers her mouth when she laughs.

Jakopie hands me a tin cup of lake water and watches my face as I taste it. "See what I mean?" he asks.

"It tastes like a lake," I tell him. Which it does—fresh and cold.

"I like tap water better," Tom says. "I guess it's what I'm used to," he adds after Jakopie gives him a disapproving look.

Etua falls asleep before dessert: Arctic berries he helped pick last summer and that Rhoda froze. He slumps over, his thumb in his mouth. Even in his Spiderman pajamas, he doesn't exactly look like your average superhero.

"Little guy had a rough day," Geraldine says as she covers him with a blanket.

"We all had a rough day," Matthew adds.

That gets me wondering about Joseph. Did he make it to the airport in time? Did the flight leave for Kuujjuaq, and if it did, were the doctors able to reattach his thumb? We have no way of knowing, since Steve took the satellite phone. If he and Joseph made it to George River in time, Steve should be able to get back to Short Lake tomorrow. If the weather doesn't stop him.

There isn't much to see through the window of the Snowflakes' tent. Just darkness. But the wind is still gusting, and it was snowing hard when we made our way over for dinner. At this rate, we may get a couple more feet of snow before morning.

None of the others mention Joseph and Steve, but I have a feeling we're all thinking about them, hoping the same thing: that they made it back safely and that Joseph's thumb is back where it belongs. I try not to remember spotting the thumb on the snow, or picking it up and wrapping it in the strip of towel.

In the distance, one of the dogs howls—a long, low howl that pierces the night air.

"Sounds like P'tit Eric," Tom says, sprinkling some more salt over his fish. "I guess he's reminding the others who's in charge."

"If there were no more Inuit sled dogs in George River, how did Steve get P'tit Eric and the others?" I ask. It's something I've been wondering since Steve told me about what happened to the dogs.

Jakopie, who's in the corner of the tent carving a chunk of caribou antler, looks up. I sure hope he won't chop off his thumb. One thumb on the ground is about all I can handle.

How could I have forgotten that Inuit sled dogs are Jakopie's favorite topic of conversation—maybe his only topic? "They come from all over," he says. "Steve looked up Inuit sled dogs on the Internet, and then he phoned up some of the people raising them. P'tit Eric and his brother came all the way from Minnesota, some of the others came from Yellowknife. Two are from Iqualuit."

"How did Steve get them all the way up here?"

"Air Inuit helped," Geraldine says, joining in the conversation. She's gathering up plates, and I hand her mine. There are only small bones left on it, so pale I can almost see through them. "The airline gave the dogs a discount on their tickets." Geraldine laughs, as if she's imagining P'tit Eric waiting at the airport, with an airline ticket in his mouth. "Steve talked the airline into it. Just like he talked some of the breeders into giving us the dogs for free. He told them it was a way to help our community."

Jakopie lays his carving down on the floor next to him. He's working on what's going to be the handle of a knife. He still doesn't look up when he speaks. "Then he and Joseph bred some of the dogs. That's how I got mine. Two of 'em are P'tit Eric's sons."

Now I'm impressed. "They are?"

Jakopie raises his eyebrows. "I hope they'll be tough like their *ataata*."

"Sons usually are," Matthew says softly. "Sometimes even tougher. Especially if the sons are born in the North. The elders say being born up here toughens dogs—and people—up." Matthew looks over at Lenny when he says this. But Lenny is busy picking a fishbone from between his teeth.

I want to know more about what happened to the Inuit sled dogs that used to live in George River. "Steve told me the RCMP killed the dogs." It's as if I can feel the letters RCMP hanging heavy in the air. At first, no one says anything. But it's too late to take back what I've said. Besides, I really want to know, even if it's a bad story.

"*Kill*'s the wrong word," Jakopie says softly. "They massacred our dogs. Came into town and shot 'em."

I suck in my breath. In my mind, I hear gunshots and dogs yelping. I shake my head to make the sounds stop.

Matthew shifts in his spot on the tent floor. "Threw gasoline on 'em afterward and set 'em on fire," he whispers.

At first, I think I've misheard him. "Set them on fire?" I say. Who in the world would set a dog on fire?

Matthew lowers his head, but he keeps talking. "Doused the dead dogs with gasoline, then threw a match at them. I was just a kid, but I'll never forget that day as long as I live." He scrunches up his nose as if he can still smell the charred remains of those dogs. "I dream about it sometimes. Even the smell comes back to me in my dreams."

"*Ataata?*" Geraldine strokes her father's shoulder.

"I'm okay," Matthew tells her.

I think maybe Geraldine wants me to stop asking questions, but I can't. I need to understand what happened up here. "Were the dogs sick?" I ask. "Did they really have rabies—like the RCMP said?" Part of me already knows the answer. What Steve explained is making more sense now: the Canadian government needed to keep the Inuit in one place. Those dogs were the Inuit's only way out. Without the dogs, the Inuit would have nowhere to go.

"There was nothing wrong with our dogs, not a thing," Matthew says. "They were good dogs, strong pullers. We depended on 'em to go out on the land." His voice sounds like it's about to break.

"That's why the RCMP killed them," Jakopie says, reaching for his carving knife. "'Cause we depended on those dogs."

"But wasn't there an investigation afterward?" I ask.

"Sure there was," Matthew says, "but that didn't change nothing. We lost our dogs, and we couldn't hunt without 'em. A lot of people went hungry after that." Now he shakes his head as if he wishes he could make the memory of those days disappear. "We lost ourselves too."

I try to picture what Matthew has been describing, but it's too awful. Worse, much worse, I realize, than what I saw happen to Tarksalik. "Did you cry?" I ask. It's a personal question, but I want to know this too. Do the Inuit ever cry?

This time, everyone in the tent looks up, even Jakopie. Lenny stops picking his teeth. His face is like a mask.

Nothing's moving—not his lips, not his eyebrows, not his eyes.

Matthew takes a deep breath. "Yup," he says, "I cried. I cried a lot."

Geraldine squeezes her dad's hand. Jakopie goes back to carving too quickly. "Killing our dogs wasn't the only thing the *Qallunaat* did to us," he mutters.

Though Jakopie didn't say "you *Qallunaat*," I'm suddenly aware everyone else is watching me, waiting to see what I'll say next.

"What else did the *Qallunaat* do?" I ask.

Lenny yawns. For the second time tonight, I notice Matthew's eyes land on Lenny. That's when I realize Matthew is looking out for Lenny. Something about Lenny worries him. The thought takes me by surprise. Lenny doesn't seem like the sort of person who needs looking after.

Now Matthew turns back to me. "It's better not to talk about some things," he says slowly.

I know I can't keep prying. Not now anyhow. Matthew opens the lid on top of the stove, and in an instant the tent fills up with gray smoke. I start to cough.

Jakopie coughs too. Like me, he must still be thinking about what Matthew just said. "Not talking isn't better," Jakopie mutters. "Just easier."

With Jakopie's voice coming out from the smoke, it feels like a ghost is talking.

TWenTY-one

I t's nearly lunchtime on Sunday, and so far no one's
said anything about packing up and heading back to
George River. It's true it's still stormy out, but if we
don't leave soon, it'll be too dark to travel today. We've got
school tomorrow, and I'm pretty sure Matthew, who works
at the gas station, has to be at work.

My mind is busy trying to figure out how we can
manage the trip back without Steve and Joseph. I think
I've got a plan. Matthew can take one dog team. Tom or
Lenny should be able to handle the other. But is it too
dangerous to travel without a satellite phone? What about
Steve? Maybe he's already on his way back to Short Lake.
We might meet up with him—unless, of course, he takes a
different path—and then what would happen? And what
about the weather? The snow is still coming down, and the
visibility is as poor as it was yesterday.

It bugs me that I'm the only one who's concerned about our situation. I keep checking my watch. 11:33:27. Every time another second goes by, I get jumpier. And the fact that all the others seem oblivious is only making me feel worse. Calm is one thing; comatose is another.

None of them seem concerned about time. Jakopie and Tom are wearing watches, but I don't see either of them check the time. The Inuit seem to be way more relaxed about time than southerners. But the question is, how do they get anywhere on time? Maybe the simple answer is they don't. Dad's students trickle in all morning, looking like they just got out of bed and not even bothering to apologize for being late. In Montreal everyone is always checking the time, worrying about being late or not getting everything done. To us, time matters.

Tom, Lenny and Jakopie are playing some dumb game they call caribou bones. It looks like the Inuit version of Pick Up Sticks or maybe dice. "Wanna play?" Tom asks me when he is setting up, trying to get a piece of caribou hide smoothed out on the tent floor,

"I don't like games."

"Suit yourself."

Then he whips out a felt bag filled with tiny bones. Who knew a caribou had so many little bones? From what I can tell, the idea is to take the pile of bones, toss them into the air and watch them drop on the floor. If one or more of the bones lands flat on its long side, the person who dropped it keeps the bone. The object is to win the most bones.

I'd say the game is right up there with watching water boil or picking a scab.

The guys are so quiet when they play it's spooky. They study the bones as if they're tea leaves and they're reading their fortunes. What I told Tom about not liking games isn't exactly true. Chris and I play cards, Texas Hold 'Em mostly, but at least we talk. These guys hardly say a word. They just study the little gray bones when they land on the caribou mat. There's some eyebrow activity, but that's about all the communication I can see. To be honest, it's a little creepy.

Some dead caribou is keeping Geraldine busy too. Right now, she's sewing beads onto a pair of doll-sized caribou-skin boots. I have to admit one thing: caribou-skin smells nice and smoky. Geraldine winces when she pricks her finger with the needle. Etua is doing a Spiderman puzzle.

The quiet is getting to me. It feels like a friggin' school library in here. And I can't even go for a walk, not with the weather as stormy as it is. I'm literally trapped in this tent with these robots. If someone at least said something like, "That wind sure is howling out there" or "Isn't this an unusual-looking caribou bone?" I might feel a little better.

"How you doin', Etua?" I ask, hoping to get a conversation going, even if it's only with a five-year-old.

"Good," he says. "Wanna help me with this puzzle?"

I'm too keyed up to work on some dumb puzzle. What I really want to say to Etua is, "Aren't you worried about your dad out in this storm?" but I know I can't. What if the kid starts to bawl? He has to be worried. But right now, the only thing that seems to be troubling Etua is that he's missing a red piece of Spiderman's suit.

Being in George River was bad enough, but being out here on Short Lake is way worse. Way, way worse. At least George River has an airport, with a plane that flies every day—weather permitting—to Kuujjuaq, and from there, back to reality. Even with all the empty space around me, I'm starting to get that claustrophobic feeling again. What if I get trapped here forever—me and a bunch of people who never talk about important stuff, like whether their friend got his finger sewn back on or whether we're ever going home? Oops, I mean back to George River.

I'm upset with myself for thinking the words *home* and *George River* in the same sentence. George River isn't my home, and it won't ever be. Even if my dad spends the rest of his life here.

"This day's sure flying by," I say at last to no one in particular. Maybe that'll clue them in to the fact that we should give some serious thought to our exit strategy.

Tom raises his eyebrows. Ahh, I think, a reaction. At least that's something.

"Can you believe it's already almost eleven thirty?" I say. "Next thing you know, it'll be getting dark."

This time, no one reacts. Not even to lift an eyebrow. The pile of bones is getting smaller. Lenny is collecting most of them. When it's Tom's turn, he scoops the remaining bones into his hands, and when they tumble to the ground, there's this look of utter amazement on his face. As if he hadn't just seen the same thing happen a hundred times in the last fifteen minutes.

Okay, I think, I've had it. "Listen," I say, trying to keep my voice calm, "are we getting out of here today or what? 'Cause if we're going, we've got a lot to do. We need to pack the fish, harness up the dogs, clear out our stuff—"

Jakopie turns his head slowly to look at me. "Relax, man," he says.

"Relax?" Right now, I'm not feeling too relaxed.

"Relax," Jakopie says again. "We just have to wait and see what happens."

I sigh. Okay, I say to myself, don't lose it. There's no point starting a fight when we should be working together to pack up. "I'm not very good at waiting and seeing," I mutter.

Lenny chuckles. "We've noticed that. But right now, we've got nothing to decide. The weather decides for us. And for now, at least, she says we're staying put."

I know there's no arguing with that, so I try to calm down and focus on the sound of my own breathing and the way my chest moves up and down with each breath. I also try peering out the crack in the tent door. The snow is still coming down hard, but now at least I can see some bushes and, in the distance, what could be the Snowflakes' tent. See, I feel like saying, it's not a whiteout anymore. But I know there's no point. These people are stubborn.

"Don't you ever get tired of all the white out there?"

Etua gets up from the floor and stretches out his forearms. He comes to stand next to me by the tent door. "It's not all white," he says, gazing out through the crack.

"Of course it is. White, white and more white," I tell him.

"That's not what my mom says. She says there's blue-white and gray-white and oak-something-white—"

"Ocher?"

Etua raises his eyebrows. "Ocher," he says, repeating the word. "Ocher-white and yellow-white..." His voice trails off.

Etua plops back down on the floor. He's had enough of a break and he wants to get back to his puzzle.

I'm still looking out the crack, feeling sorry for myself. "I just see white," I mutter.

"Yes!" Etua calls out, wriggling his shoulders with pleasure. He has found the puzzle piece he was looking for. "Maybe you hafta look harder," he says.

TWENTY-TWO

Geraldine has finished sewing the beads onto the toy boots. "Aren't they nice?" she asks, waving the tiny boots in front of me.

"Sure they're nice. They're very"—it takes me a second to find the right word—"delicate. They're very delicate... and they smell awesome."

Geraldine giggles. "I sell them at the Co-op. People hang them over their rearview mirrors for good luck. Sometimes tourists buy them for souvenirs. They do smell awesome, don't they?" Geraldine holds the boots up to her nose and inhales their scent. "My auntie smoked the caribou hide."

"Can you two not talk so loud?" Jakopie says. "We're trying to concentrate over here."

"Hey," Geraldine says, lowering her voice to a whisper, "I need to braid some wool to tie the boots together. I have to go to our tent to get it. Wanna come? I probably shouldn't go outside alone."

"Sure," I say, reaching for my parka. I'll take any excuse to get out of here. Plus, I can't say I mind the idea of some time alone with Geraldine, even if it means facing the bad weather again.

"Be careful," Jakopie says, shaking the pile of bones in his hand. "Stay close to each other."

"Just don't let him get too close," Lenny tells Geraldine.

Geraldine kicks Lenny in the butt. "Don't worry," she says. "I won't."

"And don't go letting in all that cold air," Jakopie adds once our parkas and mitts are on and I'm following Geraldine out the tent.

The wind is coming at us from every direction now, smacking our faces hard. I'm so relieved to be out of the tent, I don't even mind. Geraldine is a foot or so ahead, and it's getting harder to see her with all the blowing snow.

"We're supposed to keep close," I shout. Snowflakes fly into my mouth.

Geraldine slows down.

"So are you ever gonna come see where I live?" I ask when I catch up with her.

"You mean come to Montreal?"

"Uh-huh. There's lots to do. And lots to see." I nearly say, *Way more than here*, but I stop myself. I don't want to hurt her feelings.

"The only city I ever went to is Kuujjuaq—to see the doctor." Geraldine's voice drops a little.

"Kuujjuaq's not a city."

"Of course it is."

"Not compared to Montreal, it isn't. So do you think you'll ever come? I could show you around."

Geraldine looks around as if she doesn't want the snow to hear what she's about to say. "If I want to be a nurse, I'll need to go to Montreal for nursing school. The guidance counselor at school thinks I'd make a good nurse."

"I think you would too."

"You do?"

"Uh-huh. You didn't panic when Joseph cut off his thumb. And you didn't mind the blood."

Geraldine gnaws on the edge of her mitt. "I'm not sure about Montreal. A lot of us Inuit have a hard time in big cities. We don't fit in. Not with so many people and all those tall buildings."

I remember some of the street people I've seen on Ste. Catherine St., near the old forum in Montreal. Their straight black hair and dark glinting eyes. Some of them panhandle, some reek of booze and others look like they're hooked on drugs. These are the people Geraldine means. But nothing like that could ever happen to Geraldine.

"You'd fit in. You'd fit in anywhere."

"You really think so?" The fox fur around the collar of Geraldine's parka is dyed bright red. Her cheeks are red too.

Geraldine is smiling at me from under her *nassak*. No matter how often I see Geraldine's hair, I can never get over how black it is. Or how shiny.

I don't plan what happens next. In fact, if I had tried to plan it, it would never have happened. I'd have been too nervous, too self-conscious.

My lips find Geraldine's. Hers feel warm and soft against mine. The snow is coming down over us as if we are in one of those snow globes, the kind you shake up and down. I can feel Geraldine's lips parting. I can't believe how good kissing her feels.

"No...," Geraldine says softly. She's trying to say my name. No-ah. No-ah. Breaking it up into two long syllables, like a moan. I wish I could keep kissing her forever.

But that isn't what happens. Instead Geraldine uses both hands to push me away. At first, I'm so confused, I nearly lose my footing. What's going on? Geraldine's not calling my name. She's not moaning. Her forehead is lined in the same way it was when she was concentrating on her sewing. "No," she says again. That's when it dawns on me: Geraldine is telling me "No." She doesn't want to keep kissing me.

"No, Noah," she whispers. Her voice sounds gruff. "It's not right."

I back away. My cheeks are burning. I feel even worse when Geraldine uses her mitt to wipe at her mouth. As if she wants to wipe away all traces of me.

"Because I'm a *Qallunaaq*?" I ask her. I'm surprised that, as upset as I am, the words still come out easily.

"No, it's not that." Geraldine purses her lips together. She's not going to say any more. There are little tears—no bigger than the beads she sewed on those boots—in the outside corners of her eyes.

I don't know if I'm supposed to apologize. She kissed me back at first. I'm sure she did. It wasn't like I forced myself on her or anything. "What's wrong?" I try asking her.

But Geraldine is walking up ahead of me again. She's taking big strides that make it hard for me to keep up. Besides, I already know she isn't going to tell me what's wrong.

I don't think it's right to follow her into the tent. Not after what just happened. So I stand outside in the blowing snow, freezing my butt off and feeling like an idiot while Geraldine gets the wool.

I'm looking down at my feet, still trying to figure out what just happened—why Geraldine freaked out on me like that—and trying not to think what a mess I've made of things. My boots are big and clunky. They're surrounded by snow, and more snow is falling on them as I wait for Geraldine. That's when I notice the flakes aren't exactly white—they're gray-white—a very light gray-white, but definitely gray-white, like the edge of the sky before a summer shower. So that's what Etua was talking about! Does this mean I'm going to start noticing blue-white and yellow-white and ocher-white now too?

I want to tell Geraldine, but I'm afraid it'll sound too weird, and besides, I don't know how to start.

When Geraldine pops her head out of the tent, she opens her mitts to show me two small skeins of wool: one red, one black. "Got it," she announces. Nothing about her suggests anything at all is wrong. I can tell Geraldine doesn't want to talk about what just happened—or didn't happen.

And, for the first time since I got off the plane in George River, I'm kind of glad the Inuit are such quiet people. Because for right now, at least, I don't want to talk about it either.

"Not hungry?" Matthew says to Geraldine when she turns down the grilled ptarmigan we're having for lunch.

"Nah." Geraldine has finished braiding the wool and is sewing one end of the braid onto one of the small boots.

I can feel Matthew looking from Geraldine to me and then back to her again. I think he knows something's wrong. And even though I haven't done anything wrong, I feel bad. I've upset Geraldine.

"You're usually always hungry," Matthew says. "'Specially for fresh-shot ptarmigan. Look, I saved you the heart."

I make a point of looking away.

Matthew isn't giving up. "You need to eat," he tells Geraldine.

Lenny adds the last two caribou bones to his pile on the floor. Tom and Jakopie groan. Then Lenny looks up at Matthew. "Maybe Geraldine's just not hungry. Why don't you let me help you out with that ptarmigan heart?"

I offer to help clean up after lunch. It isn't right that Geraldine always has to do it. Matthew has filled a pot with granular snow and he's boiling it up for Labrador tea.

"You gotta dig a hole to get snow that's good for making tea. The stuff on top's too thin. You gotta dig at least a foot down to get dense snow like this," Matthew says, turning the pot toward me so I can see what he means.

I use some of the hot water for washing. There's a small bottle of biodegradable soap that doesn't lather up the way I'm used to. I try to think of the gray-white color of the snow and not the smears of ptarmigan blood on the plates I am rinsing. The wash water turns a murky brown. There are tiny specks of ptarmigan floating on top. "I guess I'd better go dump this water someplace away from the tent," I tell the others when I'm done. The bloody water is just the sort of thing I think a polar bear might like for lunch, a little soup before his main course: us.

Matthew is squatting on the floor. "The city boy is getting smarter," he says to no one in particular. It's the nicest thing anyone's said to me since I came to the North.

TWenTY-THree

I'm not exactly thrilled when Lenny says he'll come dump the dirty water with me. Dumping dirty water *on* me would be more Lenny's style. "I can manage on my own," I tell him.

"In this kinda weather, it's better to go out in pairs," he says, though I find it hard to believe Lenny is concerned about my survival. "Besides," he adds, "I need to stretch." He looks over at Tom and Jakopie, who are getting ready for another round of the bones game. "You two need some practice throwing bones anyhow."

Tom and Jakopie just laugh when Lenny says that. That makes Lenny laugh too. I guess for Tom and Jakopie, Lenny's just being Lenny. Maybe laughing him off is the best way to handle him. Lenny shrugs his shoulders and picks his parka up from the ground.

I'm carrying the pot of dirty water, trying my best not to spill any along the way. For some reason I think that what I'm doing is the opposite of what happens in that old fairy tale, *Hansel and Gretel*. Those two wanted to leave a trail so they'd be able to find their way home; I don't want some crazy stalker polar bear knowing the directions to my house.

There's one thing I never understood about Hansel and Gretel. Why did they want to go home anyhow? Their own dad sent them out into the forest to fend for themselves. In the fairy tale, the stepmother gets the blame, but it always bugged me that Hansel and Gretel's dad didn't stand up for his kids. If I were them, once I escaped from the witch's clutches I'd have made a beeline in the opposite direction from where their dad and his new babe lived.

If I was with Chris now, I could ask him what he thought about Hansel and Gretel's dad. Not much point, I figure, in mentioning any of this to Lenny. I bet he's never read a fairy tale in his life.

"Did you do something to upset Geraldine?" Lenny asks as soon as we're a safe distance from the tent. So that's why he wanted to come dump the water with me!

"No, of course not. Why would I do anything to upset—" I stop myself. I'm blabbering like an idiot, and even to my own ears I sound guilty. "I didn't do anything." Now I'm making things even worse. I stop talking altogether. It's so quiet now all I can hear is the sound of my own breathing.

"You have a thing for her, right?" Lenny asks. It's a question, but it comes out sounding more like a statement. I realize there's no point arguing with Lenny or pretending it isn't true.

Just then I catch myself doing something really weird:

I raise my eyebrows. Not on purpose. It just happens. I can feel them lifting and my eyes opening wider than before. Who knew body language was contagious? Next thing I know I'll be covering my mouth when I laugh.

Lenny watches my face, but he doesn't say anything. He walks a little farther, stopping in a narrow clearing. Lenny uses his heels to kick at the hard-packed snow. Soon he's made a decent-sized hole. "Here," he says, "you can dump the water here."

I do as he says.

"You have to look out for a girl like Geraldine." The way Lenny says this takes me totally by surprise. I expected him to make some stupid comment about titties.

"What do you mean?"

"She and her family have been through a lot." Lenny shifts from one foot to another. I can tell he wishes we weren't having this conversation. "Her big sister Sally had a boyfriend from down south."

"So her parents didn't mind her going out with a *Qallunaaq*?"

Lenny sighs. "Will ya quit interrupting and let me tell you what happened?"

"You could tell it a little faster," I say.

Lenny's eyes drop to the ground. "I can't tell a story any faster than the way I do. You'll just have to slow down and listen. If you want to know the story."

"Okay, okay, so go ahead and tell me. Sally had a boyfriend from the south…," I say, hoping that will prompt him to get on with it.

"The boyfriend, Jean-Guy, was a construction worker. He was up here on a job. Hung out with Sally every night after work. The Snowflakes even brought him winter camping sometimes. Real friendly guy."

"Then what happened?"

Lenny glares at me.

I didn't mean to interrupt. "Sorry," I tell him.

"What happened is Sally got pregnant. And Jean-Guy went back to Montreal. He said he'd be back to help raise the kid, he said he'd send money, but he never did. It's what some guys do who come here from the south. When Geraldine isn't going to school or working at the Northern, she helps take care of that baby. It's a boy. Sally wanted to call him Jean-Guy, but her parents said no way."

No wonder Geraldine didn't want to keep kissing me. Poor Sally. And I feel bad for the kid too. Geraldine's nephew. He may never get to know his dad.

Down on the ground in front of me, the dirty water has already turned to ice.

"I don't understand how a father could do something like that to his own kid," I say to Lenny when we are heading back to the tent.

"You wouldn't understand," Lenny says. This time when he sighs, it sounds like he is very tired. "Lots of people up here don't do right by their kids. Tom's dad roughs him and his brothers up." Lenny says it as if it's the most natural thing in the world.

"He does?"

I think about how my dad moved up here and how I get the feeling he's closer to Tarksalik and his students than he is to me. But I guess my life is good compared to Geraldine's nephew, or Tom and his brothers.

Lenny seems to know what I am thinking. "You're lucky to have your *ataata*. He's a good guy." From the way Lenny says it, I can tell he doesn't know what that feels like.

"What about your *ataata*?" The second the words are out of my mouth, I regret asking the question. Lenny tenses up, and I back away a little from him. This time he really might hit me.

But Lenny doesn't hit me. Instead he answers my question. His voice comes out low. But because I'm listening really hard, I recognize the tone of Lenny's voice. It isn't flat; it's sad. Sadder, I think, than any voice I've ever heard. "I haven't seen my dad since 1999," Lenny says. "He was on one of his drinking binges when he left George River. My *anaana* says it was the best thing that ever happened to us."

I know what Lenny is saying, but at first I can't quite take in the meaning. Lenny hasn't seen his dad for ten years? And his dad taking off like that—on some drinking binge—is the best thing that ever happened to Lenny and his family?

And I've been complaining about a dad who makes bad jokes and has an obsession with the weather.

I don't know what to tell Lenny. But he doesn't seem to be expecting an answer.

"C'mon," he says, "we need to get back to the tent."

twenty-four

I f you can't beat 'em, join 'em. That's why I'm squatting on the caribou hide, tossing caribou bones into the air. My quads are sore and the game seems dumb—until one of my bones lands flat. "Yesss!" I shout when that happens. It's definitely the most fun I've had all day—except, of course, for those first few seconds kissing Geraldine.

We're all playing. Even Matthew. It's not like there's anything better to do. I'm starting to feel like this day will never end, and I'm doomed to spend the rest of my life in a tent on Short Lake.

Lenny is back in the lead with about half a dozen bones in a small pile next to him.

Tom nudges Lenny with his elbow. "You're lucky with the bones today."

"Getting the bone to land flat isn't only luck," Lenny says. "It takes a little skill too." It's Lenny's turn, and when he throws the bones up into the air, I can tell from his face that he's concentrating, but relaxed at the same time. Maybe that's his trick. He's not tense. He's trying—but not too hard. Three of the little bones land on their sides. Lenny covers his mouth with one hand, but I can still tell he's smiling.

One thing I can say about the bones game: it's kind of calming. It doesn't require any batteries, and if you don't feel like talking, you don't have to. In a weird way, the game is helping take my mind off the fact that I'm trapped up here and that the girl I like is afraid I just want to use her.

"So you like throwing bones?" Matthew asks me.

I can feel the others watching me, waiting to see what I'll say. Even Etua, who's been scratching the side of his face with the bone he won, lays the bone back on the ground next to him. For the first time since I came to Nunavik, I get the feeling my opinion matters to these people.

"Yeah," I tell Matthew, "the game's okay. Better than I expected."

Etua grins.

"It's a real old game," Matthew says, closing his eyes for a second. "A good game. My grandfather taught it to me, and his grandfather taught it to him. But we weren't always allowed to play it."

Geraldine, who's sitting next to Matthew, pats his shoulder. The two of them look out for each other. Something he just said is worrying Geraldine.

"Why weren't you allowed to play it?" Etua sounds upset.

"Our teachers wouldn't let us," Matthew says. His voice drops. "That was back in Ottawa."

Geraldine is watching her dad's face.

"Was it because you didn't do your homework?" Etua asks. "My *ataata* and *anaana* don't let Celia play till she does *all* her homework."

"Not exactly," Matthew says. "Not exactly."

"You went to school in Ottawa?" I find it hard to imagine Matthew—especially a kid version of him—in a big city like Ottawa. Matthew feels more like an Inuk than anyone else I've met in Nunavik. Maybe it's because he's so quiet and because he always seems to be paying attention to things.

Matthew raises his eyebrows. But his eyes don't get wide and bright the way the Inuits' eyes do when they are saying yes to something good. Matthew's eyes look tired and sad.

It's the sadness that helps me figure out what Matthew is talking about. Why would an Inuit kid fifty years ago—assuming Matthew is in his fifties now—go to school in Ottawa? "They sent you to a residential school," I say, whispering the words.

At home, in Canadian history class, we learned about the residential school system; how the government and the churches took Native children from their families and sent them to live in boarding schools. The people in charge said it was for the children's good. But it wasn't. The teachers wouldn't let them speak their own languages or practice their own traditions. Some of the kids were abused. Some of them even died.

Madame Ledoux, our history teacher, said what happened was a shameful chapter in our country's history. She also said that Native people—and their children and grandchildren—are still paying the price for what happened, even though our prime minister made an official apology to them. Back then, I never thought I'd ever meet someone who actually went to a residential school.

It's like I can suddenly feel all the suffering inside this small tent. First Geraldine's sister and her nephew, then Tom and Lenny, now Matthew. I don't think in all my life I've ever felt so sad. Tarksalik's getting hurt was terrible, but it was an accident. Everything that was done to Geraldine's nephew and her sister, to Tom and to Lenny, and to Matthew, was done on purpose.

"That's right," Matthew says. "I went to residential school in Ottawa. No caribou bones allowed in there." He laughs, but even his laugh sounds sad.

"How bad was it?" I ask Matthew. It's probably another inappropriate question, but again, I feel like I need to know. I need to understand this world I've been dropped into. It's a new feeling for me: needing to understand what life is like for other people. Up till now, I guess, the only world I've tried to understand has been my own. I'm starting to get that the world is way bigger than that.

"It was pretty bad. I was only five when they sent me. Didn't see my *ataata* and *anaana* for five more years." Matthew sighs. "At first, I cried for them every night. Then I started to forget what they looked like. One of my teachers hit us with a yardstick if we spoke Inuktitut, and once I had to carry heavy chairs up and down two flights of stairs. All for nothing. But there were other kids who had it worse than me. A lot worse."

The tent is very quiet. Even the wind seems to have stopped howling to listen to Matthew's story. Geraldine looks like she's about to cry. I want to comfort her, but I'm afraid to touch her. Afraid she'll get upset with me if I do.

When Matthew speaks again, his voice has a faraway sound. "It's not so much what they did to me, it's what I saw them do to those other kids." Matthew shuts his eyes tight for a second. He's trying to make the pictures in his mind go away. I know, because I've tried to do the same thing when I remember Tarksalik's accident.

"Stop," Geraldine says, gulping back her tears. "Don't talk about it anymore."

Matthew looks startled, as if he's waking up from a dream. He nods at Geraldine, and now he pats her shoulder, the way she patted his before. Though I know it doesn't make any sense, I'm jealous that he gets to comfort her, that he gets to touch her shoulder. "I'm sorry," he says to her in a quiet voice. "I didn't mean to upset you."

I remember something else Madame Ledoux said after we watched the prime minister apologize on TV. "An apology," she'd told the class, "is good, but it's only a start. It's only words. What matters most is what comes next."

TWENTY-FIVE

Since his dad left for George River, Etua has been staying in our tent. Etua got to choose whether he wanted to stay with us, or with Jakopie and Roy, and I was kind of glad when Etua chose us. He's a good kid. But tonight he's kind of in my way. That's because I have plans I don't want him knowing about.

I wait till after Etua falls asleep to mention the beer. Tom and Lenny are still tossing caribou bones. From what I can tell, those two don't get bored easily.

I'm lying on my mattress reading *Catcher in the Rye*. Dad told me it was his favorite book when he was my age. I like the narrator—Holden Caulfield. He's the sort of person who says what he thinks, even if it's rude or inappropriate. I wonder what Holden would make of the Inuit. He'd probably have trouble getting used to them at first. But I think once he spent some time in the North, he'd like them. Holden hates phonies, and there's nothing phony about the Inuit.

Steve still hasn't turned up. I just hope he and Joseph made it back to George River all right and Joseph's got ten digits again. Matthew says he can tell from the bottom of the sky that the weather's about to clear, maybe even overnight. "The dogs know it too," he told us. "They're restless, and it's not a full moon."

Now, when the dogs bark, Tom says they probably smell a fox. "I'm pretty sure I spotted a furry red tail before. With any luck that fox'll be waiting in my trap tomorrow morning."

I've got seven cans of beer in my backpack. They should be nice and cold, since I left the backpack by the tent door. "Anybody here care for a beer?" I ask, as casual as if I was asking if Lenny's still winning at the bones game.

Lenny's head flies around like it's on ball bearings. His eyes are shining. "You got beer?"

"Not so loud," I say. "You're gonna wake up Etua."

"Where is it?" Tom asks, grinning.

"Right in here," I say, patting my backpack. "Safe and sound." The cans make a clanging sound as I lift the backpack from the ground.

"You mean to say you've had beer all weekend and you're only telling us about it now?" Lenny says.

"Do you want some or what?"

The bones are lying in a pile on the floor.

"Of course I want some," Lenny says.

Tom makes a slurping sound. "Me too," he says.

I slide the beers out of the backpack. There are droplets of water on the outside of the cans.

"You only got seven?" Tom asks.

"Seven's plenty."

"It's a start," Lenny says when I pass him a can. He pops it open and takes a big gulp. Bigger than I'm used to. Tom and I drink some of ours too. The beer tastes yeasty. When some dribbles down my chin, I catch it with the tip of my tongue.

"It's my dad's," I tell them.

"You stole it?" Tom says. His shoulders tense up. "What if he finds out?"

I hand Tom and Lenny each a second beer. Then I pop another one open for myself too. "He'll get over it. Plus I didn't steal it. I borrowed it. I'll pay him back—one day."

"One day when?" Tom asks.

"One day when I've got some extra beer. Maybe when I'm thirty."

Only Lenny laughs.

"Think you'll be teaching up here like your dad does?" Tom wants to know.

"You never know. Think you guys will still be up here when you're thirty?"

"I sure hope so," Tom says. "There's no place better."

"I don't know if I'll make it to thirty," Lenny says. He's only on his second beer, but he already looks a little drunk. It's the way he's holding his head, like he's having trouble keeping it upright. Maybe this wasn't such a good idea after all. But what harm can a couple of beers do?

"Your dad's a good guy," Lenny says. "A very good guy."

"You told me that already."

"Imagine not getting mad at you for borrowing his beer. Let's drink to your dad." Tom raises his beer can in the air. "Here's to Bill." Lenny and I raise our cans too, clinking them against Tom's and then against each other's. A bit of Tom's beer spills on the floor.

Tom leans down and licks the spot. Right where the spruce boughs are. "Don't want to waste Bill's beer," he says, laughing.

Lenny is eyeing the last can. "Who gets that one?" he wants to know.

"You haven't finished your second one yet," I tell him.

Lenny takes another long swig. "Wrong," he says. "I just finished it." He burps. "I can handle one more."

"Your *ataata* had trouble handling his beer," Tom says to Lenny. Then Tom covers his mouth with his hand, as if he just realized he probably shouldn't have mentioned Lenny's dad.

Lenny's eyes flash. "I'm nothing like my dad," he says.

So Lenny and I have something in common after all. "Me neither," I say. "Nothing like my dad. I don't sing in public or make dumb jokes."

"I like your dad's jokes," Lenny says. "Most of 'em, anyway."

Tom lies back on his elbows. He points his chin at Etua, who's fallen asleep face down in squatted position. His shoulders rise and fall with each breath. "Look at that kid sleep," Toms says. "Hasn't got a trouble in the world."

Lenny scowls. "Wait till he grows up," he mutters. "Just wait."

I have some more beer. The inside of my stomach feels warmer than it's felt in days. Everything feels relaxed, even my arms.

"I'm getting a nice buzz," Tom says.

"Me too," Lenny says, "very nice."

I lean back the way Tom is doing and close my eyes. Even if I'm underage, I feel like I've earned this beer. The last few days have been pretty intense. Just then, I feel something near me move, only I don't react quickly enough. That Lenny! He grabbed the last beer right out from in front of me.

"Hey," I say, sitting back up. "Give it back."

"No way," Lenny says, popping the can open and bringing it to his lips. "You can always steal—er, borrow— more from your old man."

"We could at least share."

"No way!" Lenny says again, lifting his free hand and swatting the air.

Tom is still watching Etua. "You really think he's gonna grow up and have it hard like us?" Tom asks Lenny.

Lenny burps again. Then he raises his eyebrows. "Everyone grows up and has it hard. Except maybe some of you *Qallunaat*. Some *Qallunaat* have it real easy," he says to me.

"You can't say that," I tell him. "*Qallunaat* have their troubles too. Everyone's got troubles. Hell, you just stole my last beer."

"You call that trouble? You *Qallunaat* don't know what trouble looks like. Did somebody ever kill your d-dogs?"

Lenny slurs the last word. He's definitely drunk. But I'm a little drunk too. That second beer really went to my head.

"I didn't do that," I say.

"He's right," Tom says. "Why can't you let it be, Lenny?"

Lenny sighs. Then he downs the rest of the beer. "I don't know why," he says. "I just can't." For a second, I think Lenny's going to cry. He turns to me. "So what kinda trouble you got?"

I kick the empty beer can with my heel and watch the can roll to the side of the tent. "All kinds."

"He doesn't get along with his dad, for one," Tom says.

"At least he's *got* a dad. And his dad never beat him or burnt him with cigarettes." Tom winces when Lenny says that. "He shouldn't complain," Lenny adds.

Maybe it's the beer, but I'm not scared of Lenny anymore. "You're the one who's always complaining," I tell him. "Look," I say, "I'm sorry."

Lenny's head swings around like it did when I mentioned the beer. "Sorry about what?"

"Sorry about what we *Qallunaat* did to your people." I use the word *we* on purpose so Lenny will know I'm not just trying to pin the blame on somebody else. I wasn't born when the Inuit dogs were killed or when Matthew and the other Inuit were sent to residential schools, but I'm a white guy and white guys did those things. If I were Lenny, I'd be angry with me too. Besides, who else has he got to be angry with?

Lenny doesn't say a word, but I get the feeling he's thinking about what I said—taking it in.

Lenny's rifle is lying next to him on the floor. He leans over and runs two fingers along the barrel. When he picks up the rifle, it never occurs to me he might try to hurt me.

But Tom suddenly sits up. "What you doing, man?" he asks Lenny.

Lenny props the rifle against his side. Then he raises it into the air, making an arc. He brings the rifle so the butt end rests on the floor in front of him. Now Lenny leans over; the muzzle is flat against his forehead. His fingers search for the trigger, find it.

I remember the morning after Tarksalik's accident, when Lenny used his fingers to make an imaginary gun and pointed it at his head. He's doing the same thing now. Only he's pointing at his forehead, not his temple, and it's a real gun. A real, loaded gun. My heart is pounding so hard I'm sure Lenny and Tom can hear it.

"Quit fooling around!" Tom says. His voice sounds high.

"I could blow my brains out right now," Lenny says. His voice is so flat I can't tell if he's serious or joking. "That way I'll never turn into my *ataata*."

"Don't go talking crazy, man," Tom says. "You're never gonna turn into your *ataata*."

"Give me the rifle," I say, careful to keep my voice calm in case Lenny is serious. I want to know what Tom is thinking, but I feel like I shouldn't take my eyes off Lenny. As if by keeping my eyes on him I can stop him from doing something really stupid. Once again, it's my fault. I should never have let Lenny have those beers. I should never have brought those cans up to Short Lake in the first place.

"I can't give you my gun," Lenny says. "You don't have a per…mat. I mean a parm…" He can't get the word out right. But that makes Lenny laugh, and when he laughs, the gun wobbles on the ground.

That's when I make my move. I swoop down and grab the gun. Just like Lenny swiped the last beer out from under my nose before. Now we're even. But Lenny doesn't even notice. He's still trying to say the word *permit*.

"You've had too much beer," I tell him.

Lenny looks up at me. For a moment, he looks and sounds totally sober. "I guess you're feeling sorry about that too."

TWENTY-SIX

The others are asleep, but my heart won't stop pounding. Lenny's a wild man. And the beer made him even wilder. Bringing Dad's beer up to Short Lake was a big mistake. At least Lenny konked right out. Tom too. That was probably also on account of the beer. When Lenny started to snore, I took his rifle and hid it near the back of the tent, under some spruce boughs. It'll take him a while to find it there.

I'm lying on my foam mattress, going over everything that just happened. I still don't know if Lenny was joking. But I do know suicides happen up here. Didn't Steve tell me a student from the school had committed suicide a few weeks before I arrived? I wonder now whether it was a guy or a girl, and if it was someone Lenny knew. Then again, everyone knows everyone else in George River. It must feel terrible when something like that happens. Some kid in your class is there one day, and the next day he's gone. Just like that. Dead. And you're left looking at his empty desk.

It's strange Dad never mentioned the suicide. I'll bet he knew the kid too. I make a mental note to ask him about it when I get back to George River. If I get back to George River, that is.

At least Etua doesn't snore. He's shifted so that now I can see his face. His eyelids are fluttering. If he's dreaming, I hope it's a good dream, one where he gets to be Spiderman or run with the sled dogs. I hope Lenny's wrong about Etua growing up and having it hard. Maybe things'll be different for Etua. With Steve and Rhoda for parents, Etua's life should turn out okay.

I could read, but I'm too lazy to reach for my flashlight. I prop my head up on my elbow. If I were closer to the crack in the door, I could look out at the sky, see if it's clearing. If it is, I could look for stars.

I'm going to have to do something about Lenny. I'll talk to Steve, see whether he knows Lenny is in trouble. Either way, he'll know what to do, how to help him through.

At first, when I hear sniffing, I don't really take the sound in. I'm thinking too hard about Lenny and Tom. Trying to imagine what it would be like to have a dad who walked out on me or beat me up.

It's only when the sniffing gets louder that I sit right up. Something's out there, and it's sniffing around our tent! Now I feel footsteps too. Heavy footsteps. Much heavier than Geraldine's when she was wearing those snowshoes.

"Tom! Lenny!" I hiss. Tom turns over, but he doesn't wake up. Lenny doesn't move. He's out cold, thanks to Dad's beer.

The only one who wakes up is Etua. He rubs the sleep from his eyes. "Is it time for pancakes?" he asks.

I shake my head. "Can you wake Tom and Lenny up for me? But don't make a lot of noise, okay?"

Etua raises his eyebrows. He unzips his sleeping bag and crawls over to where Tom and Lenny are sleeping. "Wake up!" he says in a loud whisper. "Noah wants you."

I'm peering through the crack. Matthew was right. The blizzard is finally letting up. Though it's hard to see anything outside except darkness, the world seems totally still. Maybe I imagined the sniffing sounds.

Or maybe whatever it was went away.

Etua isn't having any luck. I think about telling him not to bother and to go back to sleep. He's wedged himself between Tom's and Lenny's mattresses, and now he's trying to pry open one of Lenny's eyes. It's a good thing I took away Lenny's rifle.

Just then, I hear more sniffing. It's getting louder, coming closer. When I peek out through the crack, I'm confused. There's a mountain of snow out there. Only it wasn't there before. Where could all that snow have come from?

Of course, it isn't snow. It's a bear. A polar bear. Or part of a polar bear anyhow. I can't see the top or the bottom of him from here—just his giant furry white mountain of a middle. Even crouched over, he's huge.

My jaw drops, and every part of me is shaking—
my hands, my knees, even my belly. I want to speak, but
I know I mustn't. Besides, right now, I don't think my
mouth would work. I'm too afraid. My fear is pure and
cold and overpowering. It's draining every ounce of my
energy. Charlie Etok's words come back to me. "Fear can
tire a person out worse than anything else." Worse than
cold, worse than hunger. Now I know exactly what Charlie
meant.

"Tom! Lenny!" I hiss again, without turning away from
the crack in the tent. How can they still be sleeping? I look
down at the ground outside. Now I see a massive shaggy
paw. But it's not moving. The polar bear—it has to be a
polar bear, what else could be so big?—is outside our tent,
waiting, waiting.

I can't let my fear take over. I have to do something.
I try to review everything I know about polar bears. For a
second, my mind goes blank. But then I start remembering
bits and pieces from books and TV documentaries. You
shouldn't run away from a polar bear. You should stand
your ground. Polar bears are at the very top of the food
chain. They have total confidence. And polar bears can
sense fear. Maybe that's why he's here. He must've smelled
my fear from the other end of Short Lake.

"Give me Lenny's rifle," I tell Etua. My voice is shaking,
but that doesn't matter now. "It's at the back of the tent.
Under the spruce boughs. Quick!"

My hand shakes, too, when I grab the rifle from Etua.
Except for that one time when I tried to shoot the ptarmigan,

I've never used a gun. But over the last few days, I've watched Lenny and Tom hunt for ptarmigan. Aim, hold the trigger, take a deep breath, then release the trigger. Only where exactly do I aim? At the bear's heart? Or at his head? I can't think clearly. Must be another effect of the fear.

"Lemme see," Etua says, pushing against my leg so he can look out the crack too. It bothers me that Etua sounds calmer than me. He doesn't say a word as he peers out. He just sucks in his breath. I notice the polar bear has webbed feet, with five toes. And now those toes begin to move. The bear is coming closer. He can't be more than seven feet away. Maybe six. What's that he's got in his mouth? It looks like an animal carcass. Could it be a fox from one of the traps?

"Wake up!" I shout, without taking my eyes off the polar bear's toes. This time, I hear a groan and some rustling. "There's a polar bear outside our tent!" I shout.

Someone grabs the rifle from my hands. It's Lenny. He unzips the tent door and starts crawling out. I hear him cock the gun. I hope the beer hasn't affected his reflexes.

Etua and I watch from inside the tent. Lenny points the rifle and shoots straight up into the air. "He'll probably just go away," Etua whispers. "That's what polar bears usually do." But now, again, the polar bear's two huge white front paws are not moving.

He won't leave.

There's shouting from Jakopie and Roy's tent. "Lenny!" It's Jakopie's voice. "What's going on?"

The commotion has awakened Tom too. We don't need to tell him what is happening. Without saying a word, he reaches for his rifle.

"If the bear's not attacking, don't shoot right at him. You don't wanna make him angry," I hear Jakopie call.

"I'm just trying to scare him off," Lenny shouts back. "I'm gonna aim over his head now."

We hear Lenny cock his gun, and then there's the sound of another bullet flying though the air.

Etua tugs on my pajama bottoms. "*Ataata* says always aim for the paws," he whispers.

I'm only half paying attention to Etua. Mostly, I'm watching the polar bear and Lenny. The bear's still not moving, but then, all at once, he raises one huge webbed paw into the air. The paw is the size of a paddle. I'm sure he's going to swipe at Lenny or maybe at the tent. "What'd you say about paws?"

"Always aim for a bear's paws, that's what *Ataata* says…"

"Lenny!" I hiss. "Aim for his paws!" He probably knows where to aim, but I tell him anyhow.

Lenny doesn't hear me, maybe because he and Jakopie and Roy are shouting instructions back and forth. "He's got a fox carcass," one of them says. "Shoot up over his head again."

Lenny shoots, but nothing happens. Then he tamps the rifle against the ground. "Dammit," he mutters. "A bullet's stuck in the barrel. I need a knife. Fast!"

"Here, lemme shoot," Tom says.

"Get Lenny a knife. And get me the rocks," I tell Etua, who scrambles over to the corner where we keep the cooking supplies. It doesn't take him long to find a knife. "What rocks?" he calls.

"The ones you've been collecting. Give them to me."

"They're to make an inukshuk," Etua says. Still, he goes back to his mattress. His rock collection must be there.

"Come on!" I tell him. "Quick!" He presses stones into my waiting hands.

I can feel Etua's warm body behind me as I bend over and head out of the tent. Tom's shooting into the air now. Lenny is using the knife to clear the barrel of his rifle.

I take a stone and hurl it at the bear's feet; then I hurl another one and another. Etua does the same.

"Aim for his paws!" I tell Tom.

Bullets whiz through the air, just above the ground. Lenny's rifle is working again. They're doing what I said— aiming for the bear's paws. One of the bullets shatters a huge boulder on the ground, near the bear's paws. The bear looks startled, but he still won't move.

Instead he opens his mouth. The fox carcass falls to the ground. And then the bear roars. It's a terrifying sound, like nothing I've ever heard before. I can see the bear's teeth gnashing in the dark. I throw more stones until there are none left in my hand.

The bear roars again. And now, he raises his front paws. Blood oozes from one paw. It looks like he's about to pounce on our tent. If he does, we'll all be dead. Lenny will get what he wanted after all.

But then the bear hunches his shoulders together, so he's suddenly way smaller. He leaves the fox carcass where it fell on the snow, but helps himself to some of our Arctic char. Then he turns around and heads for Short Lake.

I cover my mouth with my hand. I can feel the blood rushing inside me. Lenny wipes the sweat off his forehead. Tom tries to catch his breath.

It's Etua who is the calmest of us all. "I don't think I can go back to sleep now," he says as he zips up the door to the tent. "Is it still too early for pancakes?"

TWenTY-seven

Am I ever glad to hear the sound of a snowmobile on Monday morning. It sounds better to me than the school bell on Friday afternoons, better even than the roar of the audience when Saku Koivu scores for the Canadiens. The sky is perfectly clear. There's no sign there was ever a whiteout. And, except for the bullet shells and a trail of enormous paw prints, some of them dotted with blood, there's no sign of the polar bear.

Etua and I help Jakopie feed the dogs. "No wonder the dogs were barking this morning," Jakopie says. "They must've smelled polar bear."

P'tit Eric wolfs down two fish heads straight from the bucket. Jakopie wants to hear more about the polar bear. Though he's lived in Nunavik all his life, he's never seen one. Not a live one anyway. "It's good you guys were able to scare off the bear. The elders teach us not to kill a bear unless we need the food. And we've got plenty of food."

"Will his paws heal?" I ask.

Jakopie raises his eyebrows to say yes. "He'll lick his paws, and they'll get better soon. That's why Etua's *ataata* knew to aim for the paws."

"*Ataata!*" Etua shouts when he hears the snowmobile. He jumps up and down the way he does when he gets excited. It makes me realize that even if Etua didn't act like he was worried about his dad, he must've been. I guess keeping his emotions to himself must come from his Inuit side. In the end, it's not such a bad trait. But I don't think I could do it. I couldn't keep my feelings in yesterday, when I was frustrated about being stuck up here, or this morning, when I was terrified by the polar bear.

When the snowmobile appears and I see Steve's bright green *nassak* underneath the hood of his parka, I feel like jumping up and down myself. It's partly because I'm relieved we're getting out of here, but partly, I think, because of the polar bear.

Hands down, that was the scariest moment of my life, but now I feel—what's the right word?—exhilarated. Yes, exhilarated is right. I faced my fear. And together with Etua and the other guys, I helped chase away a polar bear. Not bad for a *Qallunaaq!* And now I've got an amazing story— one I'm sure I'll tell my whole life. Just like Dad's story about spending the night on a rock ledge. Maybe stories are more important than I realized. Maybe even old Inuit legends have a point. Maybe that's why people bother to pass them on.

P'tit Eric spots Steve too, because he starts barking like crazy. Soon the other dogs are barking too.

Etua runs toward Steve. But Matthew, who has been loading fish onto his *qamutik*, reaches Steve first. From where I am, I can see the two men patting each other's shoulders. Though they don't seem to be saying much, I can tell they are communicating, filling each other in on what has happened since Steve left Short Lake.

But Etua interrupts, jumping into his dad's arms. Steve laughs and holds him tight. "Is Joseph's thumb sewed on?" I hear Etua ask.

"Good as new," Steve answers. "Mathilde got everything arranged with the hospital in Kuujjuaq. She's still down there with Joseph."

There's another snowmobile on its way. Even when I see the familiar parka and *nassak*, it takes me a few moments to realize it's my dad. What's he doing at Short Lake? Shouldn't he be teaching today? And what about Tarksalik?

I wave, and when Dad waves back, I walk toward him.

Lenny and Tom want to see him too. "Hey, Bill!" Lenny shouts. "A polar bear dropped by this morning. Your boy helped take care of him."

Dad grins and opens his arms to hug me. "I was worried sick," he says into my ear. "What with the weather and all. We've haven't had a storm like that in ages. And the temperature dipped to minus forty-two…"

"When I was a kid and we were out on the land, it got colder even than that," Matthew is saying.

For once Dad's not interested in the weather. "What's this about a polar bear?" he wants to know.

You'd think a person would get tired of telling the same story over and over, but that isn't what happens. Over lunch, I tell Dad and Steve the story of the polar bear. Etua, Lenny and Tom help tell it too.

"That bear was yellow-white," Etua says.

"I nearly shit myself," Tom says.

"You shoulda seen me when my rifle didn't shoot," Lenny adds.

I leave out the part about the beer. It's another thing I learn about stories: they change depending on who you tell them to.

"It's a good thing you remembered about Etua's rocks," Dad says, reaching for my shoulder and squeezing it hard. "Sounds like those rocks and the bullets to his paws got rid of the bear. Your mother would have had my head if anything happened to you." I know that's Dad's way of saying he's glad I'm safe.

I get to mush on the way home. "If you can help fend off a polar bear," Steve says, "you can mush." It feels a little weird at first, standing at the front of the sled, holding the sled handle. But when I shout "*Oyt!*" the dogs take off just like they're supposed to. And when the first hill comes, the dogs pull me up over it, and it's Steve and Etua who have to run alongside to keep up.

Later I take a turn on Dad's snowmobile. "Hold on a little tighter, will you?" Dad says when I'm perched behind him, my hands around his waist.

It's the nearest I've been to Dad since I was a little kid.

Dad must be thinking the same thing. "Remember when I used to read to you in bed at night?"

"Kind of. How's Tarksalik?"

"Doing a little better every day."

"Is she home alone?"

"Rhoda promised to look in on her."

We're quite a bit ahead of the dogsled teams, so Dad slows down, and then he stops altogether. Matthew and Geraldine are on a snowmobile too, following the dogs.

Dad and I get off to stretch our legs. It's cold, but the sun is out and the sky is very blue.

"So did you know the kid who committed suicide a while ago?" I ask him.

"Tim Arvaluk. He wasn't one of my students. But he went to the school. A ninth-grader." Dad rubs his mitts together. "He had some pretty serious family trouble."

"How come you didn't tell me?"

"I didn't think there was any point upsetting you. Mathilde got called to the house after it happened. Tim hanged himself."

I don't say anything at first. I just look out at the snow. Today, Nunavik looks like a postcard. But there's a lot about this place you don't see on postcards.

"There's lots of shades of white," I tell Dad. "See that out there?" I say, pointing to a small clearing with some low brush surrounding it. "Gray-white."

"I like blue-white best," Dad says. "You see that mostly around the river."

"So are you and Mathilde having a thing?"

Dad actually blushes. "I guess so. D'you like her?"

"Sure. She's good with dogs."

"And people too."

"Thanks for coming out to Short Lake, Dad."

"Like I told you, I was worried sick. Look, Noah," Dad says, and he makes a point of looking in my eyes, "I'm proud of you. And not just on account of the bear, though that was pretty impressive. I'm proud you had the guts to come up here. And that you're getting to know the place. That you're open to it."

"How come you never told me about the night you slept out on the rock ledge in upstate New York?"

Dad laughs. "How'd you know about that?"

"Lenny and Tom both knew about it. But not me."

"I guess it never came up."

"It's a good story. I wish you'd told it to me."

Dad rubs his hand along the outside of my shoulder. His touch feels good. "We've got some catching up to do, Noah," he says.

Dad laughs when I raise my eyebrows.

"You know something," I tell him, "you fit in well up here with the Inuit."

Dad looks pleased. "How so?" he asks.

I raise my eyebrows again. "You say how you feel without saying a lot."

"I do?"

"Uh-huh. You do."

Dad is still rubbing the side of my shoulder. "You could be right about that," he says.

TWENTY-EIGHT

FROM: Noah Thorpe [puckU94@quikweb.ca]
TO: Mom
SUBJECT: Re: What In God's Name Was Your Father Thinking?

Okay, Mom, relax. Calm down. Chill. I'm fine. 100% fine. I don't even have a scratch. Like I said, I'm fine. Perfectly fine. Better than fine, if you really want to know the truth.

Listen, please don't go blaming Dad for sending me on the winter camping trip. I wanted to go. Really, I did.

You know, Mom, in a way, YOU helped Etua and me chase away the bear. Dad said he told you how we threw stones at the bear's paws—apparently polar bears have really sensitive feet—well, the reason Etua and I even had stones was because we were collecting them for YOU!!! I told him about your inukshuk. Anyway, I'm writing to tell you please don't freak out. I'm at the computer in Dad's apartment.

Tarksalik is doing way better. We bring her outside now to do her business.

I guess I'm kind of getting used to life up here. Dad says to tell you he's really sorry and if you insist, he won't allow me to go winter camping again. But Mom, I hope you won't feel that way. Winter camping is pretty, well, amazing. And like I said, I'm fine. Better than fine, even. Hope you are too.

P.S. I don't want you to think it's a bribe or anything, but I bought you this little souvenir made by a guy named Elijah. You're really gonna like it, and when I'm back in Montreal, it'll always remind me of George River.

Love, Noah

FROM: Noah Thorpe [puckU94@quikweb.ca]
TO: Chris L'Ecuyer
SUBJECT: Re: Hey dude!

You won't believe what happened to me this weekend. I nearly got eaten alive by a polar bear. Swear to god. It came over to our tent while the others were sleeping. Dude, that thing was huge. At first, I thought it was a mountain. Anyway, we tried shooting into the air to scare him off. But polar bears are fearless. In the end, we had to use rocks and guns to chase him away.

Everyone in George River is talking about us. We're big news on the FM station.

Could you do me a favor and tell Roland Ipkins about what happened? And Tammy Akerman too?

Hey, you know that guy I told you about—Lenny? Turns out he's not really a Roland Ipkins type. Actually Lenny's all right now that I've gotten to know him.

You'll probably think I'm certifiable, but I'm planning to go winter camping again soon. Not this weekend, but the one after. Sure wish I'd taken a picture of that bear—but I was too busy trying to save my skin. Maybe next time.

Talk to ya soon, dude. When you write back, tell me what's up in Montreal. Guess the only polar bears you're gonna run into are on a poster—or at the Biodome!

Noah

I'm working on a composition about the polar bear. Because I've told the story so many times, it's pretty easy to write.

Tarksalik is lying under my desk. She walks with a limp now, but she can get around okay. Mathilde thinks by spring Tarksalik should be running again. "But only if you push her! The two of you coddle that dog too much. This is George River, not some health spa!"

Mathilde has a point. Things are different in George River. For one thing, dogs can come to school.

Dad's making us peer-edit our work. Geraldine is my partner. Her story's a fantasy. It's about a spirit girl who goes to seek this spirit boy. But there are all sorts of obstacles along the way: high mountains, deep rivers and an evil sorcerer.

"I sent in my application," Geraldine tells me after we've finished reading each other's stories, "for nursing school in Montreal. I've been talking about…well, you know… stuff…with the guidance counselor. She thinks I can do it."

"That's amazing."

Geraldine smiles her Geraldine smile. "I know," she says.

When I get home from school, Mathilde is at Dad's. She's buzzing around the apartment, tossing a jar of pickles from the fridge into the garbage ("How can a man keep gray pickles in his refrigerator?"), straightening up a pile of newspapers near Dad's chair ("Does the word *order* mean anything to you two?"), and pulling on Tarksalik's bad leg ("What a beautiful girl!").

Mathilde's got her own key to Dad's place. I guess they didn't want me to know at first, but it doesn't bother me at all. Even if she's a bit of a drill sergeant, Mathilde's heart is in the right place. Besides, I'm glad Dad has company. Who knows? Maybe by the time I get back to Montreal, Mom'll have found herself some company too.

"I've been waiting for you!" Mathilde tells me. "Jakopie's mother has gone into labor. It's her seventh child, so it'll probably come quickly and there isn't time to get her to Kuujjuaq. I'm heading right over. And we need your help, Noah."

"What do you want me to do?" For a second, I'm afraid she wants me to help her deliver the baby.

"It's Jakopie's dog team. Because of the high winds earlier this week he hasn't exercised his dogs in a couple of days. I said you'd take them out for him tonight."

"You said what?"

Mathilde puts her hands on her hips. It's her sign that there's no arguing with her.

"I haven't done much mushing…"

The only answer I get is a gust of cold air from the front door. Mathilde is already on her way.

Dad wants to come along for the ride. It's pitch dark by the time we've harnessed up the dogs. I'm a little nervous about taking over from Jakopie, but his dogs are so excited to be going out for a run, they don't seem to notice who's mushing.

"*Oyt!*" I shout, and the team takes off along the same route we took when we went winter camping.

"*Oyt!*" Dad shouts from behind me.

I need to keep my eyes on the team, but I can tell, without turning around, that Dad's enjoying himself.

Maybe it's because the dogs are still young, but they pull like crazy at first, and then, by the time we reach the bend where the road narrows, they're panting. Maybe I shouldn't have let them tear out of town the way they did.

Dad must notice too, because he calls out, "What do you say we stop and take a little break?"

The snow angels are Dad's idea. We're sitting out on the snow, when he bends backward and stretches his arms up behind him. Because it looks like fun, I do the same thing. I can't remember ever making snow angels with Dad when I was a kid.

We're lying on our backs when we both notice a faint pink glow at the bottom of the horizon.

"Aurora borealis," Dad says. "Just a little one though. You don't get the big ones this time of year—the ones that light up the sky like fireworks. They're produced by the collision of charged molecules from Earth's magnetosph—"

I put my hand on Dad's arm.

"You're right," Dad says. "I'll shut up."

The pink glow gets brighter and pinker. Then there are more lights—still pink—and they're not just at the bottom of the horizon anymore. They're swirling across the whole sky, like paint on a dark canvas. It's the most beautiful thing I've ever seen. And for the first time, I'm enjoying the quiet. Except for the lights in the sky, the world feels perfectly still.

"The Inuit say it's the spirits playing in the sky," Dad whispers.

I can see that. For a brief moment, I can even see Kajutaijug's stumpy legs, but then, with the next flash of pink, they are gone.

"The Inuit say you can make the lights dance by whistling loudly."

And so, lying on our backs in the snow, our arms spread out like wings, Dad and I try whistling. The cold air comes shooting down our lungs on the inhale, but the whistles come out okay.

If anyone saw us, they'd definitely think we were crazy. But no one sees us. And the funny thing is, the lights really do dance when we whistle.

GLOSSARY OF INUKTITUT TERMS

ataata	dad
anaana	mom
Inuk	Inuit person (singular)
Inuit	Inuit people (plural)
inukshuk	manmade stone landmark used for navigation or as marker for hunting grounds; literally *standing man*
Inuktitut	Inuit language
nassak	traditional Inuit woolen cap, usually with a pompom
nulujiutik	wood plank with an eye screw at one end, used for ice fishing
Qallunaaq	non-Inuit person (singular)
Qallunaat	non-Inuit people (plural)
qamutik	sled
tuuk	stick with sharp metal end, used to make hole in the ice for fishing

ACKNOWLEDGMENTS

This book was "born" in February 2007 when I traveled to Nunavik, Quebec, as part of the Blue Metropolis Literary Foundation's Quebec Roots project. Special thanks to my traveling companions Maïté de Hemptinne, coordinator of educational programs at Blue Met, and photographer Monique Dykstra. Thanks also to the rest of the Blue Met team, to the Kativik School Board and to the Quebec Culture in the Schools program. Even a writer cannot find words to thank our friends in Kangiqsualujjuaq and Kuujjuaq for welcoming us into their homes and their communities. I owe a particular debt to Isabelle Guay, my host in Kangiqsualujjuaq, for her friendship and for answering my questions about life in the North; to Nancy Etok and Gillian Warner for reading the first draft of this book; and to Mark Brazeau, who read the first and final drafts and who spent too many hours answering my questions and setting me straight. I could never have written this book without all of you. Thanks too, to the wonderful team at Orca Book Publishers, especially to my smart and sensitive editor, the very dear Sarah Harvey, for taking such good care of another project that is so close to my heart. And as always, thanks to Mike and Alicia, whose love makes all things possible.

Monique Polak is the author of eleven books for young adults, including *What World is Left*, a novel about the Holocaust. She teaches English literature, creative writing and humanities at Marianopolis College in Montreal. She is also an active freelance journalist, whose work appears regularly in publications across the country. This book was inspired by Monique's trip to Nunavik in 2007.